"I want some respect!" Alero's voice was powerful and furious in the belly of the church.

"Give me a little respect!" Her fingers struck the keys with elegant rage.

She sang with longing, sang with misery, sang with fear, beauty exploding always to spread its canopy across the breadth of her golden pain.

And the keys wept.

Wept with her and for her and for all the forlorn of the world.

PHILIP BEGHO is the author of several award-winning books. His wide-ranging interest has seen him in a varied career that has spanned journalism, banking, business, legal practice and university teaching. He has also engaged in film and theatrical production.

He now works as a full-time writer, concentrating largely on children's literature and Bible drama.

Songbird won the Isidore Okpewho Prose Prize 2003 and was shortlisted for the Nigeria Prize for Literature 2004.

By the same author

SONGBIRD

PHILIP BEGHO

Monarch Books

SONGBIRD

First Published 2002

Cover illustration: E.O. Oludimu
Cover illustration copyright: Monarch Books

Email: monarch_books@yahoo.com
Tel: +234 8060069597

ISBN 978-32224-4-9

PUBLISHED BY MONARCH BOOKS
NIGERIA

SONGBIRD

1

Mrs. Lucinda Oti glanced at Alero as she placed their lunch on the table. "I know how disappointed you must be," she told her daughter, "but it's by no means the end of the world."

Alero was silent.

She watched her mother go back to the kitchen and noticed that her mother carried her tall and trim frame with more than her usual grace. There was joy in her mother's movement. The joy that comes from unexpected triumph.

Alero dragged herself to the living room and slumped on the sofa.

A curious quiet had descended on the house. Apart from the sound of a tap running in the kitchen, Alero heard none of the usual afternoon sounds. It was as if the entire world had gone to sleep. She couldn't even hear Brova playing.

Where was Brova?

A soft breeze filled the window blinds, lifting them gently, and a dark swathe fell into the room. But the shadow soon lifted when the clouds outside sailed past the sun, releasing a flood of light.

It was cool. The efficient GEC fan, working silently overhead, contrived to keep the room in clement state.

Alero felt something hard against her back.

Reaching behind, she pulled out a toy plane from beneath a scatter cushion. One of Brova's fair-sized fleet.

From the kitchen she could hear the sound of pans being placed on the draining board. Her mother liked to do some of the washing-up before settling down at table.

Alero sighed.

She would have gone to give her mother a hand as she usually did, but not today, she decided.

No.

Not today…

In the kitchen now the squeak of the screen door opening, and her mother calling in the back garden, "Come in now, Brova – time for lunch!"

Alero stares unseeing at the toy plane in her hand, then shuts her eyes.

A bursary. A bursary to study Banking and Finance…

"Hello! Hello!" The happy baby voice of Brova as he skips into the dining room.

He breaks free from Mrs. Oti and frisks

toward Alero, his three-year-old face beaming with joy. But Mrs. Oti catches him before he reaches his big sister and takes him upstairs, saying, "We've got to wash off this mud from you and eat before the food gets cold."

Brova, Alero thought. Find me a sweeter child in all creation…

He was always thrilled to see her, even if he had been away only five minutes, and he would go "Hello! Hello!" in that heartrendingly sweet way of his.

She had planned to take him to the club for a ride in his favorite roundabout plane, but the news of her admission for Banking and Finance had scuttled that.

Alero tensed as her mother descended the stairs with a washed Brova and headed for the table.

She rose and joined them, but found herself toying with the food. She ordinarily had a healthy appetite and would eat up quickly and help her mother to supervise Brova's feeding.

But not today.

"You're not eating," her mother observed, giving her a disapproving look.

Alero took a spoonful of rice. She chewed it; chewed and chewed.

Her mother frowned. "Isn't the *jollof* nice?"

Brova made some airplane noises and Mrs. Oti turned to try and make him eat the scattered rice grains in his spoon, but he preferred them as airborne passengers.

"And you're not talking either," Lucinda Oti told Alero. "It's not the end of the world. And anyway I never really did want you to study Medicine. No, Banking and Finance is clearly more suitable for you. And you won a bursary – consider that. You should be glad!"

Alero took another spoonful of rice.

She chewed and swallowed it quickly, then

rose from the table, mumbling to her mother about not being hungry and preferring to eat later.

Her mother shrugged. "Why not go over to Tessy's and spend the rest of the day there?"

Alero nodded. "Just what I had in mind."

Brova, intelligent beyond his years, thought it a good idea too. He lost all interest in food and announced to the world that he was going with Alero to Tessy's.

Alero told him he could come but had to finish his lunch first.

"You haven't finished yours," Brova chided.

Alero began to climb the stairs. "If the stuff in your plate isn't all eaten by the time I finish changing, you shan't come."

In her room now she stands before the mirror.

She is breathtakingly beautiful.

Even without her luxuriant head of waist-length hair, which someone had once described as not-fair gorgeous, she is possessed of drop-dead looks.

None could tell at what forge her soft baby lips and trim nose, and those large almond-shaped eyes and laughing dimples, had been set onto her delicately-molded head to create the unique comeliness that was hers.

But it was her eyebrows that lifted her looks to a realm rare and ethereal.

Hers were soft hawk-wing eyebrows.

Soft, but more pronounced than her beautiful mother's from whom she had inherited them.

What she had not inherited though, was a mark on her right eyebrow, which contrived to raise one wing of the eyebrow slightly higher than the other.

The mark had come when she was eight years old, eight years ago.

She had sustained a deep cut across the eyebrow, and it hadn't healed perfectly despite a surgeon's clever stitching.

But the imperfection had given her added beauty.

Outside.

Inside, in the place where it really mattered, in the realm of her emotions, it gave her only hurt and pain.

Endless pain.

When she was anxious or bothered, her finger would travel reflexively to the mark, and she would remember the incident eight years ago and hurt all over again.

At the mirror now, her finger was at the mark.

No!

Alero flicked away her finger and set about changing. She slipped into a beige lounge skirt, then thought better of it and changed into a freshly laundered pair of black jeans.

Better suited to the red sand of Benin City, she decided.

When she rode in a private car she could afford to dress delicately, but not when she had to go by taxi and walk some distance to find it.

Surveying herself in the mirror, she was satisfied that the jeans wore well on her. But this was not surprising, for she had not only facial beauty but beauty of form as well.

She was tall and lissome, with well-curved hips and long shapely legs. She was only sixteen and already only an inch or two from the six-foot mark.

Once, as she passed her mother in the doorway, her mother had regarded her curiously and said, "Mind you don't grow taller than your father now, Alero."

She had replied, "I'll try not to, Mom."

But growing too tall was not one of her worries.

She donned a yellow shirt-blouse she had been given by Uncle Seven, the next-door neighbor.

Uncle Seven was a clothes merchant who popped in every once in a while with some choice garment for her family. The jeans had been a gift from the generous man a year and a half ago. It had been too big then, but she filled it out well now and no longer had to roll it up at the ankles.

But attractive as it was, it couldn't compare with the blue designer pair her mother had given her on her birthday, which had exquisite gold embroidery and was Alero's most-prized clothing.

Her father liked it, too, and had said it was her best article of clothing.

But she wasn't going to wear it now.

In the mirror, Alero's head shook from side to side. No physical feature of hers was a worry, not even the thought of growing too tall. But Banking and Finance was.

Banking and Finance…

Alero's face dropped. I had better get over to Tessy's now, she sighed.

Grabbing her savings, which was now enough for another CD, she went down.

2

Uncle Seven was pottering around happily in his garden when Alero emerged with Brova from the house.

She bantered with him a while, and in his usual fashion he sent them into gales of laughter.

Good old Uncle Seven, she thought, continuing down the driveway. He's ever so cheerful with not a care in the world, as though his wife never left him and he's not an ocean away from his children.

Mr. Robert Osato, bald and graying and a returnee from England, was called Uncle Seven because he had seven daughters and no sons, and because he had named his last daughter Seven Daughters No Son.

Seven, for short.

Alero remembered her father saying he had spent too long in England and had come away eccentric; did he think the poor girl was a racehorse?

Her mother had wondered too.

Uncle Seven was indeed merry mad. When Brova was born he refused to call him his real name, which was Omatosan, but insisted on referring to him as Alero's brova. Mrs. Oti said he guarded his cockney jealously, and Mr. Oti had agreed.

Cockney or not, the name "Brova" stuck.

A short rain shower had cooled the air, but the sun was peeking out now and a confetti of sunbirds chirped and tweeted from stem to stem in the luxuriant bougainvillea tree that held the compound in purple blaze.

The hedges lining the sides of the driveway were gaudy with red and pink hibiscus flowers and the birds were there too, probing blossom throats with long curved beaks.

Alero thought some of the birds well turned out in their iridescent green and blue cowls girded with purple cravats, but others, she sighed, hadn't bothered to change their modest wood-hue jackets and bleached yellow vests.

Brova, one of his toy planes in his hand, skipped merrily about, trying to catch the birds.

"I like that one," he cooed. "And that one, and that one, too! I've caught you, caught you, caught you!"

But he never caught any, and the birds went about their probing business quite unmindful of a little boy's squealing endeavors.

Down the road from the gate, Alero hailed a taxi and was happy to find only two passengers in it. She hoped the driver wouldn't pick too many others on the way and overload the cab.

As brother and sister were getting in, two girls aged about six rode by, one on a red bike, the other on a blue one.

The red-bike girl announced, "Osaz, see, I'm riding a bicycle and you, too, you're riding a bicycle."

The taxi chugged off, droning its way through the Government Reservation Area of Benin City, with Alero pondering the inanity of "I'm riding a bicycle and you, too, you're riding a bicycle."

Suddenly realizing she was doing this to divert her mind from Banking and Finance, Alero settled deeper into the cassava-smelling vinyl seat of the taxi and probed the girl's pointless statement with increased verve.

"Look! Look!" Brova cried, as the cab

clattered along Airport Road toward Ring Road.

They had just passed a pavilion of statues, a string of shops for masks and carvings and bronze heads. They were all over Benin, these roadside galleries brimming with clay and terracotta sculpture displayed against the backdrop of bronze and ebony works.

But Alero noticed that it was a particularly tall and weird work that had caught Brova's eye, and as the taxi drew away, she couldn't tell exactly what the piece was.

Was it a human figure contorted out of shape into some unknown terribly terrifying thing, or was it some unknown terribly terrifying thing reduced to the safe semblance of human form to keep the eyes of little three-year-olds from going blind with fright?

Or sixteen-year-olds for that matter?

"Where's your plane?" asked Alero, to wrench Brova's eyes away from strange and strangling sights.

Brova, his face bright with pride, showed Alero his prize possession, well clenched in his little toddler's fist. He proceeded to fly it to the sky of the cab's roof.

The taxi butted into the heavy traffic of Ring Road and the driver jostled for a suitable lane amid the ceaseless honking and creaking of horns and brakes.

Nearby a car revved impotently.

"Ah-ah – you no go follow Akpakpava?" the man in the front passenger seat queried.

Alero started. The last time she knew, a woman with a large red and green head-tie had been sitting there.

How much passenger change had taken place, she wondered, while she had been lost in thought, thinking of everything but Banking and Finance?

No, I mustn't even mention Banking and

Finance, she warned herself, quickly conjuring up the image of the girl on the bike.

Osaz, see, I'm riding a bicycle and you, too, you're riding a bicycle.

Maybe the girl had only just discovered she was riding a bicycle. Maybe she had thought it was a horse or camel. Or maybe even a cow that ate Cornflakes for breakfast, and guzzled Ribena for lunch and supper.

"You for follow Akpakpava," the man in the front seat reiterated, wiping sweat from his ebony-black neck with a tattered towel.

The driver gave him a sidelong look. "I wan go drop this fine sister for Mission Road first."

Fine sister, Alero scoffed. What use is that to me?

She switched her thoughts to Tessy.

I just hope Tessy's in. I'm sure she made it for Law; she's clever enough. Was her first choice Uniben, or was it Unilag? There are nettles in my mind. I can't remember. I wonder why her father chose to build his mansion in town and not in the Government Reservation Area where there's more space.

"See! See! They're wearing the same face and the same everything!" Brova gushed, pointing animatedly through the window.

Alero glanced out.

They were just turning into Mission Road and there by the junction, wearing red T-shirts and blue dungarees, were two teenage girls – identical in all respects, down to the cowlicks that sneaked out of their jaunty red berets.

"How right you are, Brova," Alero mumbled. "They're wearing the same face and the same everything."

Brova was beside himself. "The same face! The same face!"

"They are twins."

"Twins!" Brova repeated. "I like twins!"

He clapped his airplane gleefully as the taxi left the colorful pair behind.

What's it like to be a twin, especially an identical twin?

Alero shook her head. She had spent all her life wondering.

Brova placed his hand in his sister's. "I like twins."

"So do I, Brova."

Twins made a statement just by being, Alero thought. I must have twins, she decided. A girl and a boy. No, two boys. Or two girls. I don't know. It could be any, as long as they're twins. Tessy says they are difficult – they bring all sorts of problems into the world. But mine won't. They'll be different. I wish I had been a twin.

Tessy had a brother and sister who were twins, but they were not identical. They were two of her numerous half-brothers and sisters – the house, massive as it was, had more children and wives than it could bear.

Alero always wondered how the Osarenren family coped. But they seemed to manage well enough. The junior wives even sometimes went to Lagos to spend time with the senior wife, a Lagos resident.

Tessy was Barrister Bestman Osarenren's eldest child, and the only child of her mother, the good barrister's senior wife.

As Tessy once explained, when the good barrister's wife could not produce any other child after three very, very, very, very long years, the man deferred to family pressure and took another wife. After this taking, other takings were easy, and the barrister took and took. And the takings were fruitful.

"Mark you," Tessy had solemnly pointed out, "they all have to respect my mother. She's a Lagos cash madam and it was her money that put Dad through Law School and made him what he is."

Alero had meant to ask Tessy what exactly a Lagos cash madam was, but had never got round to it.

Dad waited seven years for me, Alero mused. And after that, thirteen years for Brova. And even if Brova or I hadn't come, Dad would never have taken another wife. Well, I suppose people are different. After all, Tessy's father is a barrister and Dad is only a policeman. But even if Dad had been as rich as Tessy's father, he would never have taken another wife. I'm sure of it. He loves Mom too much for that – and he's not just the type...

"*Oya,* sister, you no go commot? No be Cooke Road junction you talk?"

Alero started. Silly her! They had reached her stop. The New Nigerian Bank building towered green and tall on the left, and there on the right, a few paces back, was Cooke Road which they wanted.

She alighted from the taxi with Brova.

"Fine sister," the taxi driver drooled as he took his fare. He tried to squeeze her hand, but Alero snatched it away.

"Silly man! Silly, silly man," Alero mumbled under her breath. Then she thought with distaste, *Surely, I'm capable of a more severe rebuke?*

But all her well-bred tongue could utter was "Silly man! Silly, silly man," and quietly under her breath.

As the taxi rattled off, she heard the man in the front passenger seat grumble through his tattered towel-handkerchief, "All these modern girls sef!"

Alero wondered what he meant. Whatever it meant to be a modern girl, the way the man said it, it didn't seem a compliment. She was sure she wasn't a modern girl.

"Come on, Brova," she urged.

Brova was staring up at an old green story building on the left corner of Cooke Road. There was a stretch of windows on the top floor through which three mannequins posed, theatrical and lifeless.

"They are not real, Brova – just dolls."

"They are big dolls!" Brova gurgled, his eyes glued to the windows.

"That's a dressmaker's shop and those are mannequins to show off the dresses she makes," Alero explained.

Brova did not try to repeat the word "mannequins." Instead he broke into a smile and shyly cried, "Hello! Hello!"

Alero glanced up and saw a woman of mixed race at the window, smiling and waving at them.

Alero smiled back and walked off with Brova. I bet that's the dressmaker, she said to herself. Tessy says she's quite simply the best dressmaker around. And Tessy ought to know.

Her dresses are all superbly made. Most of them are bought abroad though. Gosh! She's got so many! Well, I suppose you end up having so many dresses when you have a barrister for a father and a Lagos cash madam for a mother.

"Careful," Alero warned Brova, steering him clear of a muddy depression.

You couldn't be too careful on Cooke Road. Little potholes and puddles dotted the place, and here and there a foraging nanny goat or a cavorting child crossed your path.

You also had to be careful to skirt the jagged edges of the zinc roofing sheets and other construction materials stored in the open by building merchants. This was in addition to the threat posed by the hot apparatuses of corn roasters and *akara* fryers.

And then there was the noise.

Hawkers cried and haggled, children laughed and sang, friends exchanged unbearably robust greetings, the hostile swore and cursed, and then cursed again. And from the nearby busy Mission Road came the clamor of car horns from wearied Toyotas and grumbling reconditioned Benzes.

And just here, not more than a dozen paces away from where Alero and Brova would turn right to Omonuwa Lane where the Osarenrens had their mansion, the music of a CD shop boomed loud, hard put though to drown the sawing and knocking of a neighboring carpenter's workshop.

The music shop was far from great. It was a dilapidated clutter of a place, and the music it emitted, exhaled in fits and stops by crooked doorpost speakers, was a cross, Alero felt, between a braying donkey and a mooing cow.

A large sign read, "New and Second-Hand CDs Available Here," but surely only second-hand rejects were ever traded within?

Alero indeed knew of better CD shops. Of

one in particular. The greatest little music shop in the world, she called it. Ah, yes…

"Alero!" Brova yelped before Alero could launch into reverie. He was flapping his free arm and trying to tug the other free. A bird shop across the road had caught his studious attention.

Alero yielded. "Okay, we'll go there."

There had been no bird shop there the last time she knew, only a refurbishing of what had been a small electrical store.

They stepped into the shop.

"Lovely!" Brova bleated, clapping his plane amid the chirping and flapping of scores of caged birds.

"I like this one! And this one! And this one!" Brova pointed to a dozen birds, stamping his feet in excitement.

"He likes them all, doesn't he?" A portly Lebanese man rose from behind a cluster of cages and stepped over a sack of birdseed to reach them.

"I like that one best!" Brova screamed, hopping and pointing with all his might at a bird.

Alero had seen the spectacular creature an instant before Brova, and it had transfixed her.

The bird was all red, except for the dazzling gold streaks on its wings and tail.

It was sitting still, so still and silent and lost, so red and golden and caught, in its constricting PVC cage.

"I like that one best!" Brova declared. "I like it best!"

The bird-seller had a great, happy smile on his face. "The little lad won't go home now without it, will he?"

"Yes, I want it! I want it!" Brova insisted.

Alero shook her head. "No deal. It must cost a king's ransom. It's absolutely divine!"

"It's a Tahiti Redgold," The bird-seller cooed with pride. "A songbird. It's silent till it sings.

And then it sings."

"May I have it, Alero? Please! *May I?*"

Brova was stomping in hand-wringing disquiet now.

"But I can't afford it," Alero protested, her eyes riveted on the Tahiti Redgold.

The bird-seller's grin broadened. "You can have it for next to nothing."

Alero gave him a disbelieving look, and the man explained that he had only opened for business minutes ago and Alero and Brova were his first customers.

"And I can't let the little lad's heart break, can I?"

He brought the cage down and emptied the water that was in a little watering tray inside. He put in a small bag of free feed and reeled off instructions on the bird's care.

Alero laughed. "But I can't afford it!"

"Please, please!" Brova shrilled.

The Lebanese looked at Alero with astute eyes. "How much have you got there?"

Alero unclipped her purse. "I was actually going to buy a CD – an original one, mind you – still, I can't imagine that what I have will do."

"Let's see." The man took the notes she fished out and regarded them inscrutably.

Returning two, he said, "I'm cutting things fine, but I can't leave an astonishingly beautiful lady on the streets without any money."

Alero knew she had a bargain of bargains. "W-why, thank you!" she stammered.

With a cage in one hand and a frisky three-year-old in the other, Alero bolted from the shop before the man could change his mind.

Tessy's gatekeeper was up the lane making purchases from a stall, but he noticed the twosome and waved as they trooped into the compound.

Surprise! All the Osarenrens' cars were gone,

except for two or three SUVs.

Alero went into a small panic, fearing no one was in when she needed so desperately to talk to Tessy.

"Alero Oti!" hollered an excited voice from behind, and Alero turned to see Tessy barreling her way from the other side of the house.

She dumped the cage with Brova and hurried to her friend, embracing her with relief.

"Oh, Tessy, for a moment I thought you were out! No one seemed in."

"They've all gone to Mom's in Lagos! Only Dad and I and one wife stayed behind."

She hadn't gone with the others, Tessy explained, because she was waiting to hear if she made it to the university.

"Oh Alero, I made it for Law – made it to Uniben! I just got the letter this afternoon! I'm going to be a lawyer! *I made it!*"

She kissed Alero and hugged her in a bear

hug, then hugged her twice again to near-death, the sturdy seventeen-year-old lass blissfully unaware she had the strength of an Olympic shot-putter.

She turned to Brova.

"Oh Brova! *Brova!* I made it! I made it! Is that your bird? Where did you pinch it? It's *brill!*"

But for the restraining cage she would have hugged the bird, certainly to death, in her powerful joy.

Sweeping up the cage, she ushered her guests into the Osarenrens' glass and concrete mini-palace.

Alero kept her eyes on the Tahiti Redgold with her heart in her throat, for Tessy was a champion tennis player and was swinging the cage like a storming racquet.

They lounged in one of the three marbled living rooms downstairs – Alero's favorite, for in a corner was a white Steinway piano.

Tessy cleared off the lawn tennis trophies on an ornate stool and plunked the cage on it.

"And you," she nudged her friend, joining her on a sumptuous ten-seater sofa, "did you make it for Medicine or Banking or both? You brain box!"

Alero was completely joyless when she replied, "Banking and Finance – Unilag."

Tessy studied her. "You sound a bit glum. I had no idea you were so keen on Medicine."

"I'm not."

"Then shouldn't you be happy you made your first choice?"

"That's just the point," Alero moaned. "I'm neither interested in Medicine nor Banking and Finance."

"But Alero, those were your two choices!"

"Not mine. Mom's and Dad's. Mom was ever talking of Banking – I don't know where she got the idea. While Dad..." She laughed ruefully. "Dad not only wants me to become a doctor – he wants me to become a brain surgeon!"

She gave Tessy a desperate look. "They filled the forms for me! No one asked me what *I* wanted – they just filled in what *they* wanted!"

Tessy was silent. She stared at the fountain in the middle of the room.

Alero's eyes traveled to the fascinating luxury, impressed as the water leapt and fell in the changing colors of concealed rainbow lights.

"Alero, I never realized –" Tessy started.

"I know," Alero broke in. "It wasn't something I could talk about."

She glanced at Brova. He had taken the cage from the stool and was meandering toward the fountain.

"Brova, mind you don't get too close!" Alero warned.

"Sometimes, Alero," Tessy told her friend

slowly, "I think you're too deep for your own good." She looked hard at the shiny marble floor. "I've known you all these years, all through school – but there are times I think I hardly know you."

"Brova, take the cage back to the stool, please," Alero ordered.

Tessy let out a long sigh. "Alero, just what is it you want to study?"

Alero looked away.

She looked across to the Steinway piano, standing quietly, regally, gleaming pristine white, glistening gloriously.

A dreamy faraway look came over her eyes, and she said quietly, almost inaudibly, "I'm going to be a singer."

She heard Tessy clear her throat and shift uncomfortably, but she didn't look her way.

Brova skipped over and pointed at the cage which he had labored to put back on the stool.

"The bird wants some water," he informed his sister.

"How do you know?"

Brova grinned. "I just know."

Tessy got up. "I'll fetch the water – and shouldn't we have a drink along with birdie? What would you like, Brova?"

"Fanta, please!"

"Orange Fanta for you – and blackcurrant for Alero as usual?"

Alero nodded. "Thanks."

"Goodness! So I know something certain about you?" Tessy strolled off to fetch the drinks.

Rising to her feet, Alero sauntered to the Steinway. It was a battle restraining herself from touching the majestic instrument, but she let the wishes of Barrister Osarenren prevail.

How a man could purchase so magnificent an instrument and forbid the playing of it never ceased to baffle her.

The good barrister forbade even the touching of it. Tessy said he valued it only as a work of art, as one would prize an old master – and great paintings should never be profaned with human fingers, should they?

Alero studied the gleaming piano top. Not a speck of dust.

Someone must do a bit of shining everyday, she surmised, and he must do some touching to do it. How honored cleaners are – the things they get to touch!

"What shall we call my bird?" Brova had slunk up to her.

Alero kept her gaze riveted on the piano. "Songbird."

"Songbird?"

"Yes, Songbird."

"But he's in a cage!"

Alero wondered what that had to do with

anything. She gave him a sweet smile. "He's a songbird, so we'll just have to call him Songbird, won't we?"

"Can he sing?"

"Yes."

"Can he sing like you?"

Alero caught her breath. Whatever made Brova ask that? When had he ever heard her sing?

"Yes," she said. "He can sing like me." A little tear stung the corner of her eye.

Brova scampered off crying, "Songbird! Songbird!"

Tessy sallying in, stopped short when she heard what Brova was calling the bird.

She trundled meditatively to Alero and said, "We called you that once, didn't we?"

Alero didn't answer. She kept staring at the piano.

Tessy shook her head. "There are too many

things about you I don't understand."

She stalked back toward the kitchen. "I just came to say there's peppered chicken warming in the microwave."

Alero crossed the immaculate floor to her seat.

Songbird.

Yes, they had called her that once.

Her mind went back in time. A year ago. Form five. The microphone was in her hand. It seemed so light and so heavy.

And as if it was coming from another room, she heard the titters, and the titters became jeers and boos, and she wondered who they were booing, and she looked at the microphone in her hand, and she saw the microphone clearly through her tears, and she thought, "I had no idea a microphone was so light. So light and so heavy."

And the boos engulfed her. It was a year ago,

in form five.

Alero sat in reverie until Tessy returned.

"Brova," said Tessy, placing a tray on a stool, "here's the water for your bird – and something nice for the rest of us."

Alero picked up a drumstick. "Thanks." She stared at the chicken piece. "If I could only get Mom on my side before Dad returns." Her gaze was disturbingly abstracted.

Tessy sipped her drink. "He's away on tour again?"

Alero nodded. "In Irrua." She sighed and shut her eyes momentarily. "You know, I'm so glad I didn't make Medicine. I'd never have been able to persuade Dad off it for Music."

"With all the A's you got!" Tessy shrilled, but Alero wasn't listening.

"I've got to go to music school," she was saying, "and really learn to play the piano – and really learn to sing! I'm going to sing a thousand songs!"

Tessy plunked down her glass. "Alero say – what's wrong with Banking and Finance?"

Alero gave her friend a long stare, then quietly put down her uneaten drumstick.

"Yes," Tessy insisted. "What's wrong with Banking and Finance?" Alero made to speak but Tessy continued, "You didn't even offer music – you dropped it in junior school!"

Silence sat heavy between the two teenagers a while, then Tessy said, "Alero, you got the best results in Emotan International – probably one of the best results nationwide – and you have the chance now of training to become a highly-paid banker, but all you have in your head is this airy-fairy nonsense about singing."

Alero said nothing and Tessy brooded a bit and then gushed, "Alero – you should have put in for Law! I can see us both in wigs and gowns – the famous formidable pair – heaping up laws known and unknown before an amazed judge and running breathless rings around our befuddled learned friend on the other side! Just think of it: little us, sending the gallery giddy with champagne arguments! Oh Alero! *Alero!*"

And she went on and wove a colorful tapestry of heroism and noble deeds at the bar, which no doubt the barrister, her able father, had primed her to from nappy-swaddling infancy.

"And I think I shall specialize in arguing jurisprudence," she concluded. "Don't ask me what it means, but it's certain to mean something clever – really clever!"

Alero watched a bridge of light stretch through the window to link the rainbow lights of the fountain with the strong sun.

She turned to her friend and said quietly, "You sound so excited about what you're going to do, Tessy."

"I couldn't be happier and more excited,"

Tessy agreed.

"Don't you think, dear friend," Alero told her, "that I, too, deserve to be happy and excited about what I shall have to spend the rest of my life doing?"

"Oh Alero, Banking and Finance is a splendid course! Bankers are rich and important people. And you could study Law later, you know. That would make you a financial law expert. Dad says some of the richest lawyers are financial law experts!"

"Songbird isn't drinking his water," Brova said suddenly, skulking by Alero's shoulder.

Alero turned and gazed at him strangely, as though she couldn't get her eyes to focus.

"Songbird isn't drinking his water," she muttered, "because Songbird is sad."

"Why is Songbird sad?"

"Because..." Alero's mouth felt dry. She swallowed. "Because Songbird has lost his song."

"If I teach Songbird a song will he be happy?"

Alero shrugged. "Maybe."

Brova's eyes rolled as if he was ransacking his three-year-old memory for just the right song. Then he ran off to his red and gold poorling.

"Songbird," he cried frantically, "I'm going to teach you a song!"

"Songbird…" Tessy batted her eyes.

She turned to Alero. "You sang once, Songbird, only once, but it was so out-of-this-world. It was like hearing an angel sing!"

She fell silent, and then with an urgent frown, her elbow swinging in the motion of a goring bull, she stuttered, "B-but that doesn't change things, Alero! You're too brainy to make singing your career. For people like you, it should be a hobby only. It's like me taking up tennis just because I'm awesome at it."

She chuckled. "Ridiculous! How utterly and completely absurd! Tennis – when I could have the prestige and respect of being a lawyer!"

She tossed back her head and roared with laughter. "To think of being a singer when you could be a dignified banker – it's so silly really, so impractical, just a dreamer's Friday foolishness!"

Alero groaned in her seat.

At the windows, the sun blazed through the fine silk nets and suddenly died.

This cloud that hovers, Alero thought, *is dark, dark, dark. Grave, beastly and dark.*

She rose to her feet. "Come, Brova; we've got to be on our way."

3

It was dark, but a moonbeam floated in through the curtains to give a little cheer to the night.

The bed creaked as Alero turned to look at her watch on the bedside cabinet. She had to strain her eyes in the half-light to make out the time.

Ten minutes to one.

She lay back and, through the quiet and stillness of her room, listened to the night sounds of GRA Benin.

In the distance a whirring sound.

A water pump or perhaps an air conditioner, Alero concluded. Or maybe some over-heated ballistic refrigerator, but certainly not ours downstairs. It could even be a generator somewhere far away where there's a power outage.

No, it's too thin. Too thin even for a generator far, far away.

Beyond the whirring sound she could hear the drums.

She had heard the drums almost all sixteen years of her life. Whenever she woke at night, they were there. But they had never really scared her, these night drums of Benin. They were too far away.

They are at the edge of night, she thought. *At the edge of night.*

Suddenly from outside came a clang. Then farther away, another. And from a different direction, yet another.

Night watchmen, Alero reflected, announcing the hour with rod on pole. Announcing, too, their watchfulness to anyone who might care to know.

She raised herself again to look at her watch.

1 AM.

The watchmen are bang on time. She smiled. No, I rather think they're clang on time.

She lay back and continued to distil the sounds filtering in through the open window, which had sturdy bars and a mesh screen to stave off human mischief and bloodthirsty mosquitoes.

Why am I doing this? Alero wondered after identifying twenty-seven different sounds.

It's because I cannot sleep.

I've been lying wretchedly on this bed since I arrived home from Tessy's. And my stomach is growling but I cannot eat. My eyes are smarting but I cannot sleep. I'm tired but my limbs pulse with energy. I'm cold but I'm hot! O God, I'm miserable!

Her finger traveled to the mark on her eyebrow.

My life is confused. I don't know where to turn. And Tessy, my own best friend, *my own best friend...*

Something flapped downstairs. It was the first clearly discernible sound she had heard in the house. She held her breath.

There it was again!

"This needs investigating!" And with the recklessness that comes from misery, she got up and donned her housecoat.

Opening the door gently, she crept out on tiptoes, thankful for the night lamp in the landing and careful not to wake Brova or her mother in their rooms.

Halfway down the stairs she froze.

Robbers!

Could it be robbers?

She was going to scream but the flapping began again.

Ah – she knew what it was!

Songbird!

She had quite forgotten the bird in her misery.

Oh Songbird!

She leapt down the stairs and plunged into the living room.

She flicked on the lights but the bird flapped madly, so she doused them and switched on only the ones in the dining room.

"Bird in a cage, how so forlorn you are," she whispered, staring deep at the bird which had now become quite still. "Your eyes are sad, so sad and weary."

Then out of her depths a flow of words took shape, and Alero uttered them as though she had always known them:

Bird in a cage, how so forlorn you are!
Your eyes are sad,

They are worn and weary with weeping.

Bird in a cage, how so silent you are!
Your throat is still,
It's chained and fettered with pining.

Bird in a cage, Songbird, my Songbird!
I know your pain, your ache, your shame –
For you and I are lame.

Bird in a cage, caged bird, my caged bird!
I know your heart, your harm, your hurt –
For you and I are caught.

She did not sing the words, she uttered them merely, but they came out with the force of that strange musical power that was locked in her throat.

And Alero remembered and wept.

She remembered a day, a day she needed so badly to forget, and wept.

She was eight years old. She was in the

bathroom. Her father and mother were down-stairs, her father watching TV, her mother in the kitchen.

Her mother came halfway up the stairs and called to her, "Alero, don't spend ages in there, your food will get cold." And she called back, "I won't be a sec, Mom."

She had indeed spent much too long in the bathroom, but not without reason...

A group from Lagos had given a musical performance just before close of school. It was riveting, and pupils and teachers had rapturously applauded, with a female soloist drawing a standing ovation.

As Alero piled into the school bus at the end of the show, she overheard a teacher say to a colleague, "If only one of our girls could sing like her – we'd be famous!"

Back home Alero had playfully thought in the bath, "Maybe I can sing like her."

And for a laugh she had tried to mimic the girl.

To her utter surprise, she remembered the girl's song word perfectly – and she had never heard it before.

But even more surprising – she could make her voice do all the fascinating things the girl did with hers.

In fact she seemed to be singing the song more arrestingly than the girl!

What a wonder!

Was she really singing so beautifully or was her mind being partial to her? The girl had been daring with her voice, and Alero, to mimic the girl, had been as daring.

Dare she dare more?

Why not?

Alero pushed a note a little higher and it went easily. She pushed it higher still and it went splendidly. She pushed it higher and higher and it went and went and was tuneful still.

On a whim she brought it crashing low and saw that it was dramatic and melodious.

In this low range she quickly shifted notes and was amazed at the deep purring beauty that issued from her.

Suddenly she went high, then plummeted, caught a middle note, went high again, soared there for a while, came down, down, down, exploded aloft, then suddenly stopped.

She had rearranged the song at her whim and had never once got off key.

There were tears in her eyes.

Sweet beautiful heavens, I can sing! I can sing! I can sing! I can make my voice do anything! Anything!

She tried again and it was the same.

Again and again.

She was going to do it one more time when her mother called.

The spell was broken. Doubts began to creep in. Could it be true? Could she really sing? Maybe it was all in her head. It had sounded incredibly beautiful inside, in her head, to her, but how would it sound to others?

She hadn't sung loud at the top of her voice. She had sung high and low, but not loud. It couldn't be true. It was too beautiful for words.

No, she really couldn't sing that well. She was only eight – only eight, what did she know?

She soaped and sponged herself quickly, eager to go downstairs to sing to her father and mother – *they* would tell her if she could really sing.

She raced down.

Her food was in a covered dish on the table, her mother in the kitchen, and her handsome father, tall and powerfully built, was watching TV in the living room.

She lifted the lid to peek at dinner.

Golden Glory fried plantains! And beans! How mouth-wateringly delightful!

Should she eat before she sings? No, that wouldn't be a good idea. The food might cloy her voice. She would sing first, then reward herself with the golden pieces of plantain fried the way only Mom could.

But how should she start the singing? Could she just say, "Hey, Mom! Hey, Dad! Guess what? I want you two to be good parents now and sit down quietly together – very quietly now, my darlings – and listen to me sing"?

The TV will have to be switched off – but how do I do that with Dad so rapt in the seven o'clock news that I could walk on my head and chew the carpet and still stay unnoticed?

The news ended.

I just might catch Dad's attention now.

As Alero stood still, waiting for courage and wisdom to give life to her trembling intent, a filler faded up on the screen.

Alero couldn't believe her eyes. There on the screen was the girl who had sung at school!

And she was not being interviewed or anything like that – no, she was singing the song, the same song she had sung at school, the one Alero now wanted to sing to her parents!

Alero didn't know when she sat by her father on the sofa, listening enthralled. She barely noticed that her mother had joined them.

Father, mother and daughter – sitting together in deep thrall on the sofa.

The song ended and the girl took a bow.

"That was the version made popular by the great Flamingo," Alero barely heard the girl say. She barely heard, because she, Alero, was talking.

She was saying, "When I grow up I'm going to be a singer like her." And Alero heard her father say, "What did you say?"

"I said when I grow up, I'm going to be a singer like her."

She was going to say more but never did.

Maybe she was going to ask her parents to listen as she did a version of the song. Maybe she was just going to say, "Mom, Dad – I'm so glad you're my Mom and dad – I love you so."

But she never spoke.

There was a sudden explosion in her face and something stone-hard rammed into her right eyebrow.

Shock!

Rude shock!

Daze. Cold daze.

And then the pain started coming.

And blood.

Slick red blood, hot, running over her eye, blinding her in one eye, blinding her, blinding her, running all over, and she could taste it in her mouth; the blood was in her mouth, it was running down her nose to her mouth, she could taste it in her mouth, like salt, tasting in her mouth, it was running down from her eyebrow, mixing with her tears to sting her eye, it was stinging her eye, the pain, surging, rising strong, surging, surging, rising strong, face aflame, a deep piercing ache in her head, the pain, screams, screams, her mother's screams, her mother's hands over her, the pain, and her father's finger, her father's massive finger waving menacingly in her face, his face gnarled in a knot of fury, and he was saying, "Never ever! Never ever! *Never!*"

And the pain was a flame in the inferno of her mother's hysteria, in the holocaust of her father's raging; it was a fiery geyser shooting through her temple from three sides, shooting, shooting, until all began to go black, began to go black in sections, as though night was falling in patches, as though the light bulbs of life were failing progressively from the outer windows of her vision to the clustered center of her skull.

The last she saw, the last she remembered, was her father kicking and smashing the TV to smithereens.

She was only eight.

She didn't know what she had done wrong. No one told her what she had done wrong. No one explained, no one said anything.

No one said why.

Why there was no longer to be a TV set in the house, or why her father kept their only radio locked in his room, or why she was never to give or go to parties.

No one said why.

Why there was to be no music.

No music in the house.

Why no one was ever to sing.

Eight years ago.

The years had passed quickly and slowly, and

slowly and quickly, and you couldn't tell now that there was once a deep cut across her face which had borne huge and fierce stitches.

You couldn't even tell that the point where one wing rose higher than the other was where her father's jagged ring had smashed deep into her face, smashed deep as he struck her with that ferocious blow of his.

It gave added beauty to her face, for sure it did.

But what about the ugly hook it gave to the aching question in her mind – to the why?

The *why* that twisted itself in tortuous knots in the caverns of her soul.

Eight years.

Eight years and no answer.

A few months after the incident, she had gathered enough courage to ask why.

"Mom," she had said as she and her mother were having a late Sunday breakfast, her father away on police duty.

"Mom…"

Her mother had not answered but had stared suspiciously at her, her teacup dangling precariously in the air.

She's just a step away from being frightened, Alero had surmised. *She knows what I want to ask. She knows – but how?*

"Mom?"

Her mother rose from the table.

"A-Alero," she burbled, "there's a birthday cake to be collected in a couple of hours and I haven't even started!"

And that had been the end of the matter.

Three years later, after a nightmare, Alero brought up the incident again. This time without timorous dally.

"Mom, you know when Dad hit me –"

Her mother cut her short. "You must forget the past, dear. You must forget the past."

Mrs. Lucinda Oti tossed aside her rolling pin, washed her hands, untied her apron, and marched upstairs, leaving a bewildered and distressed Alero to meditate the bleak walls of a petty baker's kitchen.

Alero had never asked again.

But she had never forgotten either.

How could she?

Can one forget the pain that forms the bars of one's prison existence?

The event changed, to the deepest depths, the relationship she had with her parents.

Where once she had roamed the field free and easy with her mother, no territory forbidden, she now roamed free and easy, but only in the outskirts of a fenced-off area that was quite simply the entire field.

She only, alone, by herself, in the quietness of her thoughts, could go into the corralled area.

What joy was there in this? What joy in being

alone?

As for her father, she had loved him once with affection, now she loved him only with fear.

She had loved him with fondness, now she loved him only with duty.

She had loved him easily once. Now she loved him warily. There was a gulf between them, and look as she might, there was no bridge in sight.

The event had changed her character too.

Whereas she had once had the innocent unrestraint of a carefree child, now she had learnt to withhold, to ponder, to suspect and to fear.

She had learnt that the world held a harvest of darklings to its breast, so, in step with the world, she had learnt to thresh in the dark barn of furtiveness.

And this had put a wedge between her and her

peers.

And from her solitude and quiet pondering had come a ripening of her intellect beyond her years.

This put a further wedge and left her to cut a solitary path through life, alone in her whys and wherefores.

Alone in the pain that sealed her in silence.

Alone in everything that mattered.

She had been silent and had sung only once in all those years. Only once and they had called her Songbird for it.

Songbird!

Alero rose from her reverie.

She glanced at the clock on the wall. 3 AM. She turned back to the red and gold bird in its PVC cage.

Maybe you want to sleep, bird. But you won't sleep while I'm watching you.

Aloud she said, "You haven't sung yet,

Songbird. Maybe you'll never sing."

The Tahiti Redgold stared at her, its eyes sad, its eyes liquid, its wings clipped, its wings furled, its throat locked, its voice disdaining to utter a single note.

"Goodnight, bird. Maybe you'll find sleep and maybe I will too."

She extinguished the lights and went back upstairs.

But she couldn't find sleep.

She placed her pillow on her head and pressed it down hard, but sleep would not come.

She turned on her left and then on her right, but it was no good.

She dug herself into the sheets and wrapped herself all up until she felt like a half-starved Egyptian mummy with a pair of toothaches.

Grimacing, she muttered, "Not very funny."

She freed her face and stared at the dark, her eyes brimming with night and sleeplessness.

Maybe I should count the sounds of night again.

No, she thought, I think this calls for a little night's music.

She got out of bed, pulled out a red suitcase from her wardrobe and fished out CDs hidden beneath a pile of old clothes.

The suitcase was one of her two "music cases."

The other music case was a black one, and from this she brought out a small CD player which, like the CDs, had been kept beneath camouflaging clothes.

From the collection of CDs she selected three that sported Ms Aretha Franklin beaming in three different smiles.

As Alero, comfortably ear-phoned, lay back on her bed to listen to the marvel of Aretha Franklin, her mind went back to the first time she heard the voice of Aretha.

She was fourteen years old. The school bus had gone for repairs, so at the close of school she had hopped into a taxi with several other day students.

As the cab puffed and sweated its way along Itohan Road, a strong and magnificent voice suddenly shattered the afternoon sky.

"Stop! Stop!" Alero screamed.

Leaping out before the taxi creaked to a halt, she raced to the shop where the voice in fearsome power was producing music to halt the spheres.

Ah, the greatest little music shop...

She became a frequent visitor at the shop and was given a special corner where she could sit and listen undisturbed to Ms Franklin.

"Aretha sings with a power that transcends time," she explained to the storekeeper when he wondered why she was not more interested in the singers and style of the day.

"She sings with the power and soul with which I shall one day sing," she had added.

Suddenly conscious of herself, she had whispered modestly, "If I could sing, that's how I would like to sing."

Over the course of eleven months, Alero plundered her savings to buy five Aretha CDs – yet she had no equipment to play them on.

Sometimes at night she would lock the door of her room and gaze at the CDs, remembering in her head the music of each CD and pining for the miracle that would produce a music player.

She waited and waited – oh what a waiting! But twelve months after the acquisition of her first CD, wait's end came screeching to her bus stop and she arrived in school to find posters everywhere announcing a talent contest – first prize, a CD player.

Second prize what?

Alero had no eyes for it.

Her schoolmates tittered when she entered for the competition, the cattier ones remarking that it was a talent contest not a beauty competition, mind you, Alero.

On the eve of the contest, she stopped by at the greatest little music shop.

As she sat down in her accustomed corner to listen to the Aretha number she wanted to sing, she thought, "Dad forbade music in the house. I must confess to disobedience, Dad, for tomorrow I shall bring music home."

Anyone watching her may or may not have seen her lips move as she added, "I'm disobedient, Dad, that I may live."

The next day came and it was time for her to go on stage.

As the master of ceremonies handed her the microphone and strode off, all Alero saw before her was a sea of doubtful faces.

She took a deep breath and began the Aretha

Franklin song, but she hadn't gone beyond a few notes when she stopped.

For a second there was utter silence. Then the titters came. And then the jeers and boos.

But before any missiles could follow, another bout of silence fell, for the audience had noticed that Alero was in tears.

The master of ceremonies hurried to her. "Don't be a cry-baby now, come on; singing isn't for everyone, you know."

He took the mike from her and announced to the hall, "We'll have the next contestant, please. Kindly give Ms Alero Oti a round of applause for having the courage to try."

Amid perfunctory hand-claps, the emcee tried to shoo Alero off, but the gorgeous teenage girl was going nowhere.

Wiping her tears, she spoke calmly into the microphone, "I haven't even started."

The emcee blinked, then waved off the

wannabe that had shuffled noisily over.

"Ms Oti appears to be made of rather hardy stuff," he chuckled. "Let's give her another try."

Alero held the microphone firmly, and with a voice as strong as unshuttered light, she said, "I stopped singing because I decided to change my song. I apologize. I cried because I remembered something very sad that happened when I was eight. I apologize, too, for that."

She paused, the silence pulsing, the audience taken aback by the confident, self-assured manner of the fifteen-year-old.

"I was eight years old when I last sang this song," Alero told them. "It was the first time I had ever sung it. It was also the first time I had ever heard it."

She took a deep breath and began to sing.

She sang slowly, from deep within, her voice powerful in the school hall. She remembered again the night of blood and her finger went momentarily to her eyebrow, her voice trembling with heavy melody.

Then embracing the lyrics with gentle grace, she gave wings to her voice, sending it up to the roof of the school hall where it spread and rolled and flowed.

When aloft it had wrought melodious mysteries, she brought it down, down, down to the floor and kept it there in a gentle flood to wash the feet of her amazed audience.

Then, as on a whim, she seized her voice and took it to the middle air, unfurling it there to display its rainbow colors.

Suddenly, when the lyrics denoted urgency, she sluiced the song into a sliver of sound and sent it slicing through the hearts of her slack-jawed audience.

The people gasped as one, then gasped again in a scattered serrated catching of the breath.

Alero retrieved the sliver, plucked the barb to

her, and spread her voice like a canopy over the heads of her stunned and gawking schoolmates.

A little while, a little parade of vocal marvel, and she folded her voice and let silence reign.

But not for long.

Her voice, untrappable, unstoppable, slipped out, this time soft and tender, caressing and cosseting incredulous souls.

The people sighed.

The people moaned.

The people moaned again.

And Alero stopped.

There was not a sound. There was no one, you would think, not a soul, in the hall.

Oh heavens, Alero thought, *years and years – and nothing has changed! I can make my voice do anything!*

She took her bow with tears in her eyes.

It was when she began to head offstage that the applause came.

It hit her, hit her rudely, hit her gladly, then hit her sweetly. Everyone was on their feet, clapping with all their might.

Long minutes and the applause did not let up.

"Encore, *Songbird!* Encore!" cried the crazed audience. "Encore, encore!"

Backstage, Alero dabbed a little tear from her eye. *Songbird! They had called her Songbird!*

The master of ceremonies came wheezing to her. "You've got to do an encore or there will be a riot! Come on!"

Alero went back on stage.

"Perhaps you'd like another version," she suggested, and the hall fell silent. "This version is how I think a friend of mine would do it."

And she began to do the song the way she imagined Aretha Franklin would do it. She did it to a quick beat and gave it a sharp touch, then slowed it down and gave it soulful depth, and then caught the quick, rocking beat again.

There was great surprise as the audience wondered how a song that had been done so reverently could be given this rocking, dancing touch.

But soon everyone caught the beat, and the wonderers wondered no more, but gave dancing rein to their limbs, and soulful nods to their heads.

And those who could do so took the cue from Alero and uttered soulful cries, soul corroborating soul on the feverish parquet floor of the school hall of Emotan International Secondary School in Benin, as dusk donned its cloak outside, and the stars reared themselves to peep at a sad and happy world.

And Alero did not let up.

She improvised and kept improvising until she suddenly remembered she was in a contest and others had to be given a chance.

Lowering the tempo until the dancing

stopped, she shut her mouth and began a moan that seemed to come from a depth deeper than any place within her fifteen-year-old frame.

Her mouth was closed, but her throat went into uncloistered vibration, issuing full-bodied sound from her bosom and the lip-less air around her, which seemed to have suddenly become full-lipped.

Sweet heavens, Alero exulted, *there's a strange and wonderful instrument in my throat! All I have to do is think, and it does what I think!*

Suddenly she opened her mouth – and sound, deep and arresting in full-winged melody, exploded to the roof, ramming it fiercely, deeply, then bouncing to the floor and shooting up again to keep the unrecovered roof stunned and sagging.

Back and forth, back and forth, to the roof and floor, melody and harmony, thundering from the dazzling teenager's throat in fierce unforgettable congress, disported and danced till everyone's tears fell shamelessly to feed the panting school floor.

Then Alero reined in her voice, bowed and sashayed offstage.

"One year ago…" Alero muttered, rising from the bed. "One year ago, I sang for my life."

She took off her earphones to go to the bathroom but was impaled by a sudden piercing note from downstairs.

Songbird!

She stifled a cry.

Songbird!

She leapt out of the room and sprang downstairs.

Songbird was singing at last!

The bird saw her but kept singing, and Alero drew a chair to the cage to listen.

She listened attentively as though trying to

84

interpret the song of the red and gold cageling.

After a while she sighed and said, "I know what you're saying, bird. I understand."

She closed her eyes and followed the song into regions of non-human wanderings.

She saw, through the iris of the bird, forests green to tears with mono-wealth, and forests raging loud with many-colored foliage; she saw valleys and hills, swamps and fields, crashing waterfalls, lakes unknown to man, bald and gray rocks, black ones, too, bold and virile; and virgin streams, virgin springs, virgin wealth…

Across a beach with sand white as snow, the bird flew and alighted on a rock and lifted its eyes to the sun.

Alero understood. The bird was lonely.

Opening its mouth to wail, the bird rose with its cry and all its hurting, rose higher than any creature had ever done and stared into the face of the sun.

There it wept.

Then the bird was in an orchard, a fruitful grove, and it cocked its head to the right, ever to the right, listening, it seemed, to something unheard.

Suddenly Alero distilled a song like the bird's drawing nearer and nearer, and the Tahiti Redgold cocked its head restlessly, pining for its mate.

Then it raised its wings to fly to its mate, but the wings could not get it airborne.

Alero groaned. A cage! The bird was caught in a cage!

Out of the foliage appeared the bird's mate, her song undying in her throat. The caged bird gazed at its mate, the end of its search, its pining; the bird gazed, gazed at hopelessness, gazed at despair, gazed at despondency, gazed at loss.

And wept.

And the bird with the song undying, the song unfulfilled, the song unconsummated, understood, and killed her song, killed it with the same threnody that had cut her heart in twain.

And men came with great and raucous laughter to take the caged bird away.

Suddenly Alero realized that Songbird had stopped singing.

She waited, hoping it would say more, but the bird only regarded her with its liquid eyes and kept *omerta*.

Alero rose from her chair.

"You'll kiss the face of freedom again, bird," she vowed.

Going up to Brova's room, she roused him and took him downstairs.

Standing him before the cage, she said, "We've got to set Songbird free, Brova. It's your bird; you've got to do it."

Brova took a little look at the bird, wobbled

on his feet, yawned, and ambled to a chair. In but a beat and a half, he was curled up asleep in the chair.

Alero smiled and turned to the cage.

"Tomorrow, bird," she said. "I promise you tomorrow."

Lifting Brova gently to her shoulder, she carried him back upstairs.

4

Alero pulled back the bolt and pushed the gate open. It was a small black gate and it was hot from the morning sun.

She felt dizzy. Tottering into the compound, she reproached herself for not having breakfast before setting out to see Rest Peacefully. She hadn't touched a meal in almost twenty-four hours and the morning's fierce sun was not helping matters.

And she should have slept.

Yes, she should have slept.

She had begun to feel sleepy in the morning but had got up determined to go early to see Ms R.P. Smith.

Ms R.P. Smith, or Rest Peacefully, as the girls called her, or Restie for short, was the principal of Emotan International Secondary School.

Alero, tossing and turning all night, decided she needed to talk to someone who could persuade her parents to let her enroll in a music school. Her erstwhile principal seemed just such a person.

Alero kept her movements slow as she made her way toward the front door, knowing vertigo was only a step away.

Only vertigo?

Munro, Ms Smith's stealthy Doberman, unknown to Alero, was also only a step away.

When the dog sprang, Alero didn't know what hit her. She fell on her back, her face up, staring straight into the horror of clashing incisors and splashing saliva.

She fainted.

The feel of water on her face brought her gazing into the comforting eyes of Rest Peacefully who, with the gardener's help, got her into the house.

"I'm awfully sorry about this, Alero," the principal squawked the umpteenth time. "Really, really sorry."

She was relieved to find no bites on her former student, only minor bruises to which she applied old-fashioned iodine.

When Alero took the tea she had brewed, Alero held the cup with both hands to keep it from shaking. But it shook nevertheless.

"I can't imagine what got into Munro," Ms Smith repined. "He's never been this stroppy." Her embarrassment gave color to the English paleness of her face.

Alero sipped her life-saver in silence.

Looking shrewdly at the school-leaver, the schoolmistress said, "Alero, are you all right – I mean apart from the episode with Munro?"

Alero placed her cup down.

She was silent a moment, then proceeded to tell Restie why she had come.

"But you dropped music in junior school!" accused Ms Smith when Alero was done.

Her tone was much the same as Tessy's but the accent was different, was like butter in hot potato sauce.

Alero said nothing, but a veil came over her eyes, and her mind went back to a certain time in junior school.

She had won a scholarship into the privileged Emotan International and had found to her unspeakable joy that it was compulsory to take music in the first two years of junior school.

Enrolling to play the piano and guitar, she attained a proficiency that left her tutors astonished. But she never sang.

She continued with music in her third year and had every intention of offering it in senior school.

But something happened.

She borrowed and took home one of the school guitars, and as she was ascending the stairs to her room, it was suddenly snatched from her.

Turning in shock, she found her father, whom she had thought was out, smashing the guitar at the foot of the stairs.

"Dad!" she screeched. "It's only for my music lessons! I won't sing! *I won't sing!*"

Her father stormed at her and she only escaped by fleeing pell-mell to her room where she locked the door in terror.

Dashing up, her mother managed to coax her father away from the door he was on the verge of kicking down.

The next day, it was as though nothing happened. As with the punching incident, no one explained anything.

Her mother just quietly went out and bought a new guitar and, with Alero in tow, took it down to school and handed it to the music master, informing him that Alero was dropping music.

The tutor never learned from mother or daughter why the most promising student he had ever known was dropping music.

"Alero, you're miles away," chided Ms Smith.

Alero recoiled to attentiveness, and Restie droned on.

"I was saying you've got the jitters – school leaving jitters – I see it all the time. After twenty years of hobnobbing with you girls, I can tell when I see the jitters."

The principal smiled patronizingly.

"You were a first-class student. I haven't the slightest doubt, love, that one day you'll sit behind a first-class desk in a first-class office."

She recounted stories of former students who, in the public schools of England and the three continents where she had taught, had indulged in escapist visions and dreamed of being international fashion models and film stars.

But of course the madness was never long-lasting; they turned from their idle frivolity and did the sensible thing of becoming bank workers and secretaries.

Alero looked through the window at the sky.

The sky seemed three yards down the road. She wrested her eyes from the mammoth heavens and lowered her gaze to the floor of the veranda.

A redneck lizard snapped up a gnat buzzing around its head, did seven perfect press-ups on Restie's veranda, and hugged the warm floor proudly.

Alero had no eyes for redneck pride.

She gazed back at the sky, then got up and left.

*

In the taxi Alero felt a tightness around her chest. She had decided not to go home, but to Tessy's. After the disappointing encounter with Rest Peacefully she needed to talk to someone – *she just had to talk to someone.*

The constriction around her chest tightened and Alero shut her eyes; shut it tight. It's the cage, she thought. It's the cage! I'm caught in a cage and the cage is squeezing me to death!

Oh, to be free, to be free like Songbird!

She remembered Songbird flying into the sun.

At daybreak she had brought a sprightly and alert Brova to the cage.

"Songbird has got to be free," she told him. "He's got to be let out of the cage."

Brova glanced at the bird and then at her.

"Why?"

"Because his mate wants him – his wife, you know. They just got married, but he got caught and was taken away."

She waited for him to say something but Brova just gawked at the bird.

She decided to make the story more plausible.

"Songbird's Mom is in tears. She's looking for her little darling everywhere and Songbird wants to go home."

Brova gave her a curious look. "Is Songbird little like me?"

"Yes, he's little like you and little boys shouldn't stay away from their moms, should they?"

"But little boys don't marry, do they?" There was a little crease of worry on Brova's brow.

Alero coughed. "Well, are we going to keep Songbird unhappy in his cage or are we going to let him go home to mom?" Quietly under her breath, she added, "Or to wifey, or to both mother and wife."

Brova blinked. "Will he come back sometime to say hello to me?"

"If you ask him politely, he just might."

Brova whispered to the bird then looked up at Alero and grinned.

"He said he lives far away but that when I grow up and have an airplane, I can fly over to see him in his country."

"How nice of him," Alero chuckled. "Be sure to take his address now. Come on, let's get this cage out to the patio."

She gave Brova the honor of opening the cage, but the bird wouldn't come out. She thrust in her hand and brought it out.

Flapping onto the veranda, the Tahiti Redgold gazed at them with sad liquid eyes.

"Go, Songbird – *go!*" she urged.

The bird hopped a pace away and gazed at the sun, then at Alero and Brova, then back at the sun.

Opening its beak, it let out a piercing cry and rose with its cry, straight as an arrow, into the eye of the sun.

"Bird on the wing," Alero gasped, "how you rise in freedom!"

A tear pricked the corner of her eye, and a flow of words slipped her lips:

Bird on the wing, how you rise in freedom!
The world is yours,
You deafen the morning with song!

Bird on the wing, what liberty you know!
Your world is wide,
You garland the heavens with joy!

Bird on the wing, Songbird, my Songbird!
Oh for your wings, your flight, your span –
But here I am enchained.

Bird on the wing, freed bird, my freed bird!

Oh for your song, your trill, your thrill –
But who will set me free?

"Cooke Road junction! *Oya!*" the taxi driver shouted.

Alero collected herself and tried to fish out her fare, but her brain and hand were in disagreement.

"Sister, I beg – pay me my money and come down!" the driver snarled.

When Alero finally could do what her mind wanted and gave him his fare, he growled, "You no know where you keep money – na so you go cook soup no know where you keep meat for inside."

Alero tried to hurry out of the cab, but as before her limbs couldn't match the fuzzy command of her brain.

The driver bared his teeth to bite again, but a sudden ray of understanding reared him to leash.

"Sometime im no well," he whimpered.

But couthness squatted only on momentary haunches.

"You tink say because you be fine girl you fit no well inside my motor?"

He gave a guttural laugh, pleased with the excellence of his renewed coarseness, jerked his back-to-front baseball cap down hard, scraped the peak severely to rub in the bristles of his attack, unchained his gear, and roared off.

Alero walked quietly down Cooke Road.

There's something wrong with my limbs, she said to herself. *And I feel so light-headed. But I mustn't let go, I mustn't drop down in a heap.*

She halted at Omonuwa Lane, a few yards from the Osarenrens' house.

What do Tessy and I have in common? she queried. *Tessy lives in a practical world and I in a dreamer's Friday foolishness.*

Turning on her heels, she staggered away.

At the bottom of the lane, she glanced across to the bird shop.

The shopkeeper noticed her and waved, but she didn't wave back.

He beamed a great smile at her, but she didn't smile back.

He beckoned. She hearkened.

Hearkened over to the bird shop.

The portly Lebanese tried to make small talk, asking about Songbird and Brova, but he stopped short when he noticed the look in Alero's eyes.

And she had begun to busy herself trying to open the door of a cage.

His next words were in no small-talk voice. "What are you doing?" he bellowed.

Alero's fingers were working feverishly. "As you can see, I'm trying to open the door of this cage."

"*Why?*"

"So the bird can fly away and be free like Songbird."

The shopkeeper decided a man had to know when to ask questions and when to take action. Lurching toward her, he tried to make her let go of the bird she was de-caging.

Alero went berserk.

She elbowed him, kicked him, screamed and railed.

"Set the birds free!" she screeched. "Set the birds free! They don't belong in cages! Set the birds free!"

The man resolved to subdue her and cages went crashing down, birds squawked, wings whacked cages, furious feathers flew, sweat splashed, curses screeched, screams rent the air, the walls, the ceiling – until Alero, all her strength spent, collapsed in a heap on the floor.

In a half-faint she felt fresh hands and heard new voices, girlish voices, sweet voices…

Opening her eyes, she saw two girls wearing the same face.

She tried to tell them they were wearing the same face and shouldn't be doing that when Brova wasn't around, but fatigue left her mumbling incoherently.

The twins raised her to semi-recline and fanned her, while the Lebanese bird-seller soothed her brow with a wet flannel.

Soon Alero felt better and the twins led her from the shop into a taxi.

"I hope the next time I see you, you're wearing your red T-shirts and blue dungarees," she told them, though the taxi had taken her well out of earshot.

She added solemnly, "We'll have to pass a law forbidding twins from wearing anything but red berets, red T-shirts and blue dungarees."

O heavens, what am I saying, she suddenly lamented. *What have I just done?*

5

There's nothing wrong with me, Alero told herself, as she stood at the doorstep back home. All I need is some sleep.

She opened the door and tramped into the living room.

"Hello! Hello!" Brova cried, running to her and expecting her to sweep him up as she usually did.

Alero didn't have the strength.

She ruffled his hair. "Big sister has got to go find some sleep."

Her mother was at the dining table rolling and cutting dough.

Alero mumbled greetings but her mother, clearly crestfallen, didn't acknowledge them.

Somebody has told Mom of the scene at the bird shop, Alero thought in panic. *Somebody has told her!*

"Brova, give this letter to your sister," Mrs. Oti ordered.

Alero took the letter and noticed it bore the imprint of the University of Benin.

I shouldn't open this letter, she told herself. *I shouldn't.*

But she did and it informed her that she had been admitted to the University of Benin to study Medicine on a full scholarship.

Her mother's sadness flamed into accusation. "That's what you've been waiting for, isn't it?"

Alero didn't answer. She just let out a groan and collapsed into an armchair.

Her mother's brow creased. "I went to Uncle Seven's to phone your father. He was beside himself with joy but said it was for you to decide if you wanted Medicine or Banking – Of course, I know he only said that to please me."

She gave the dough a series of quick chops with her knife.

"He'll be returning tomorrow to see about the admission." She hesitated, blinked, and said, "You can't stand the sight of blood, can you? Look Alero, Medicine is no career for anyone who's squeamish – I keep saying it! You want to be a brain surgeon? *A brain surgeon? Please!* Do you know what a brain surgeon does?"

She gave a hollow laugh.

"Besides, by the time you finish, you'll be too old to marry – I was married at eighteen, you know. And doctors are on call night and day – what kind of life is that for any sensible female? I must take you to Lagos to have a chat with

Mrs. Banifo. At eight forty-five she's ushered from her company house into a company car and chauffeured to the bank – ten minutes away. She works just ten minutes away from home, you know. At 5 PM after a jolly good time presiding over tea and snacks in that air-conditioned executive suite of hers, she's chauffeured back home. Now that's what I call a sensible life for a woman!"

Mrs. Lucinda Oti did not let up as she extolled the virtues of a banking career in the top league.

But Alero had no ears. *Tomorrow,* she thought. *Tomorrow, Dad returns. Tomorrow, judgment day.*

Her finger went to the mark on her eyebrow and she had visions of the night of blood and battering.

Struggling to her feet, she said, "Mom, I'm going out for a walk," and wobbled off.

She walked down quiet roads and lanes deep in the GRA, traipsing through places she had never known.

She was in a daze, her night without sleep and her lately unnourished body robbing her of any awareness of the life around.

Bees hummed in the sun, dragon flies zipped, lizards did press-ups, a grand-daddy butterfly, huge and proud, with a moth-like head and peacock wings, danced flirtatiously around her; two rickety cars hooted past, an airplane droned far overhead, a palm-wine tapper's crooked bicycle clattered by, the tapper but a shrunken elf atop his one-and-a-half-wheeled contrivance; a truck-pusher, his haul of fresh timber a creaking mountain of fragrant wood, rolled elephantine biceps past, and a mangy dog, suspicious neck outstretched, trotted warily away from the distracted girl, assaying unsuccessfully to keep its paws unscorched by the sun-baked red soil of ancient Benin.

But none of these things registered in Alero's mind.

"Tomorrow, judgment day," she mumbled to herself. "*Judgment day!*"

She walked and walked, not knowing whither she walked, and in the outskirts of her mind the thought alighted that she was lost.

She cared not a hoot.

Taking footpaths unknown, byways strange and ominous, lanes thick and green with caterpillar-ed vegetation, she walked in a tired daze, but with a resolve only fear and pain could bestow. Then, unexpectedly, she found herself in familiar territory fifteen minutes away from home.

She had walked in a circle.

Trudging a reluctant path home, she came upon St Joseph's Church, a small Catholic parish to which she had never before given more than a passing glance.

"Maybe the priest can help me," she mumbled, turning into the church premises.

There was no sign of anyone on the grounds, so she walked straight into the building.

A priest was standing close to the altar, his vestment ghostly white in the depths of the church.

She marched up to him. "I want to sing."

The priest, a young bespectacled man aged about thirty, looked at her quizzically. "Who are you?"

"I want to sing," she said again.

"You want to sing?"

"I've got to sing," Alero clarified.

"You've got to sing," the priest repeated.

"My father wants me to be a brain surgeon and my mother wants me to be a banker, but all I want is to sing. I want to sing a thousand songs."

"Are you well?"

Alero looked forlornly at him. "Can you tell Mom and Dad to leave me alone and let me be what I want to be?"

The priest adjusted his glasses and drew nearer to the stricken girl. "You seem troubled."

Alero looked at him wretchedly. "My mother wants me to lead a sensible life with tea and snacks in a banking suite. How can I sing a thousand songs doing tea and snacks and Filofax?"

The priest shook his head. "You seem very, very troubled."

He tried to lead her to a pew but she shrugged him off.

"I just want to sing and my parents won't let me!"

"What's your name?"

Alero did a double take. There was a piano by a stained-glass window and her eyes zeroed in on it.

"Are you a Catholic?" the priest asked.

Alero pointed to the commanding instrument. "Is that any good?"

"Perhaps if you said a confession you would feel better," the priest suggested.

Alero hurried to the piano, raised the lid and tried a chord.

"No, *please*," the priest admonished.

Alero tried another chord.

"No, you mustn't!" the priest exclaimed.

Alero was satisfied with the new chord. She closed her eyes and played, her head swaying in pain, her bosom heaving.

Then her mouth opened and Aretha Franklin's *R-e-s-p-e-c-t* rolled out, deep with unrelenting soul.

"I want some respect!" Her voice was powerful and furious in the belly of the church.

"Give me a little *respect!*" Her fingers struck the keys with elegant rage.

She sang with longing, sang with misery, sang with fear, beauty exploding always to spread its canopy across the breadth of her golden pain.

And the keys wept.

Wept with her and for her and for all the forlorn of the world.

"No, *please!*" the priest protested. "You mustn't! You *mustn't!*"

But Alero played and sang and wept in a stunning storm of fury, with no ear for the *mustn'ts* of the world.

And the reverend gentleman took a seat, adjusted his glasses and listened to the marvel that had suddenly dropped from the blue to vivify his church and bejewel the rosary of his saintly experience.

Tears filled his eyes, and then suddenly all the music, like the nothing of this astonishing girl with no existence in his erstwhile world, ceased, and the priest stumbled to his feet as the girl fled down the aisle.

"Miss! *Miss!*" he called, desperate to know the teenage wonder.

"I didn't come for any confession, Mr. Priest!" Alero yelled over her shoulder before disappearing outdoors.

She ran all the way home, tears peppering her face, her feet striking the ground with anguished exhaustion, her breath stabbing the air, propelled by chest-pounding constrictions.

At the front door was Mr. Robert Osato waiting for her.

She leaned breathlessly against the wall.

"You heard?" the neighbor asked. "You've been told?"

Alero stared at Uncle Seven bewildered.

It was evident the usually jovial man was the bearer of distressing news.

What had happened?

Alero tried to speak but couldn't manage it,

her breath insufficient for even so unmomentous a task.

She slid to the ground as Uncle Seven was inserting the house key in the lock.

He even has the key to our house! What has happened? What has happened to Mom? Where is Brova?

"What...what h-happened?" Alero managed as Robert Osato helped her in.

"No one knows exactly," replied the man. "But he's alive. The car's a write-off though. Your mother set out immediately for the motor park with Brova. She has the address of the hospital."

Dad!

Dad has been in an accident!

Alero collapsed face down on the sofa and began to sob.

Then sleep came suddenly.

Merciful sleep.

6

When she awoke, light had thickened and night could be sensed crouching in the wings, poised to ambush dusk.

She had slept for two hours.

Only two.

Drifting to the kitchen, she made herself a sardine sandwich and returned nibbling it.

I'll help myself to a more filling meal later, she promised, sprawling on the sofa and sinking into the bliss of nothing. Then she took hold of her mind and scouted the situation.

If Dad has been in an accident and is in hospital, he won't be coming home tomorrow – I have more time to find an answer to the course of my life; more time...

Relief flooded her veins.

She rose and stumbled to the kitchen. Things were looking up; she could afford to indulge in a good munch. She would eat well; very, very well...

Then it hit her. It came in waves, the remorse, rolling upon her like nausea.

She staggered back to the living room and plopped into an armchair.

My father has been in an accident and all I can think about is me! How wicked can a girl get?

She broke into sobs, self-reproach an unmerciful steamroller over her troubled mind.

I must be the vilest thing living! My father is in hospital and I'm glad he's not coming home.

Glad – why? Glad because I'm thinking of me, me, me!

O me! O me!

For long minutes she sobbed, and then the scene at the church suddenly flashed through her mind.

She pondered, then wiped her tears and climbed to her feet.

"I need to do a confession," she announced to the meager furniture in the room and vamoosed.

Fifteen minutes later, when no Catholic church was in sight as she tramped along, she realized she had taken the wrong turn.

About to retrace her steps, she noticed a church just up ahead. It wasn't St Joseph's Church, but it was a church. Should she venture there?

She cast a glance at her watch. 6:45. Light was thickening relentlessly.

One church is as good as another, she

119

decided, trudging up to the church.

She glanced at the signboard. *Three Circle Pentecostal Church.* Milling about her were people evidently there for some evening event.

Alero scanned around to see if she could spy a priest.

Hmm. No one in white vestment. But over there, that man – he has the air of a church official.

She hurried to him. "Excuse me, sir, where can I find the priest?"

"The priest?"

"Yes, I want to do a confession."

"Oh, you want to get saved."

"No," Alero told the man. "I want to do a confession."

"You want to confess your sins to God?"

"Yes, I'm in bad need of a confession."

The man beckoned to a nearby colleague talking with some head-scarfed women. "Could you spare a minute, Brother Hope? This young lady needs to be prayed for – she wants to get saved."

"No," Alero protested, "I just want to do a confession."

Brother Hope and his female companions hurried over, and the Pentecostal acolytes placed their hands on Alero's head and began to pray at the top of their lungs.

Alero got frantic. "Take your hands off me! I just want to do a confession!"

They didn't take their hands off her.

One of the ladies knotted her scarf tighter and told Brother Hope, "I think she needs deliverance."

They stepped up their prayer. Other bystanders joined in.

"Let go of me!" Alero screamed, struggling hysterically. "Let go!"

Cunning came to her. Going limp in a false

faint, she suddenly wriggled through the milling feet of the crowd and sprang away.

For the second time that day, she ran all the way home from church.

Safely upstairs, she tore off her clothes, plunged into the bath and shampooed and soaped herself, determined to get rid of the hands that still seemed to cling to her.

"I thought there was something wrong with me!" she wailed. "But it's not me – it's the entire world!"

But as she wallowed in indignation, she couldn't shake off the feeling that something good had happened to her.

Not knowing what it was, she felt even angrier. She lurched downstairs, made herself a large and fierce dinner, and furiously ate it all.

"I'm not alone," she reassured herself, pushing away her empty plate. "I'm not alone in this madness. The world itself is mad!"

She was sipping Ovaltine when Robert Osato came in with a small pile of magazines.

"To keep you company," he told her.

He was glad she had given herself a good supper and all seemed well in the circumstances.

Alero frowned. "The circumstances are even knottier than you think, Uncle Seven."

The balding neighbor leaned forward in his seat. "Tell me, forlorn child."

Alero hesitated, hedged, said she had confided in enough people, said everything she had tried hadn't helped, said she wasn't going to tell.

But she did. And it came out in a torrent of words – words sometimes thick with emotion, sometimes thin with hysteria. But she told him – told him of her dreams, her frustrations, her desperation, her despondency; of the wretched thing life had become, of the hopelessness of *being*.

Uncle Seven listened raptly, remaining utterly silent until she had finished.

He let out a long sigh. "Don't make the mistake I made, Alero."

Alero's glance at him was questioning, but he didn't speak and a cloud of sadness settled over him.

Finally he groaned and explained that he had once been on the verge of training to become an architect, but had let it go because he had been a dreamer like her.

His dream, his scourging ambition, had been to design clothes whose beauty would make women weep.

"But it was a dream greater than I, Alero," he moaned, "and I wound up an importer and exporter of garments."

He gave her a grim look.

"I then switched dreams and desired to have a son I would raise to become the greatest fashion designer in the world. But I ended up having seven daughters who knew only how to wear clothes, not make them. And my wife absconded because she despaired of finding me a son."

Alero looked away, her eyes moist with pity.

Who would have thought that the jolly old clown was such a sad man?

"Why didn't you go back to Architecture?" she asked.

Misery clouded Robert Osato's eyes. "It was too late in the day. The sun had blazed and died, and evening was nigh – I had missed my life."

His gaze fell to the floor as he reflected.

"Dreams are diverting," he said after a long moment. "They are but dreams, just dreams, empty and useless."

Alero sat back in her chair. "Wait a minute, sir, some people *do* become acclaimed singers and fashion designers, wouldn't you say?"

"Those are a different breed of people. They

are like the songbird."

"The *songbird?*"

Alero was startled by the coincidence of allusion.

Osato's mouth worked silently, then he said, "The songbird asks no one's permission to sing. It just sings. It sings to survive. It doesn't sing to impress itself or anyone. It sings or perishes."

He shifted in his seat.

"I did not design and I did not die. If you do not sing, Alero, will you die?"

Standing to go, he muttered, "Humanity is clothed in failed dreams. It is the story of our lives."

Alero had never heard him speak like this, had not even thought him capable.

She stood up to let him out.

"Forget the madness, Alero," the man advised. And with a wry smile, he added, "It doesn't worth."

"It doesn't worth?" Alero was puzzled.

Uncle Seven laughed. "I once knew someone who used to say that. Instead of saying 'it's not worth it' he would say 'it doesn't worth.' I found it quite droll. You see, Alero – in my graying years, I have become a clown, with a daughter called Seven Daughters No Son."

Alero forced a smile, knowing better now how much the funny man's eccentricity concealed pain.

She let him out, but soon had to reopen the door when he knocked again.

"You must be careful, child," he said in the doorway. "Your father is a fine man, but he disapproves of music. Beware of people who disapprove of music."

He shuffled away, his years telling their truth on his frame like never before.

Alero retreated to the sofa, her finger finding the mark on her eyebrow.

She hadn't told Uncle Seven of the night of blood.

*

Stretched out on the bed, the keys to her music cases ringed around her finger, Alero wondered why she was feeling so relaxed.

She was so relaxed that she knew she would sleep well tonight. Perhaps it had to do with that article she had read.

One of the magazines Uncle Seven brought featured the ten most successful female singers in the world. Reading of their sorrows and pains, Alero had noticed that if it was about troubles, hers could admit her to the rarefied club of these extraordinary people.

They had all endured a tough and bitter struggle and understood to their depths the meaning of that mystical word *Perseverance.*

"I will persevere," Alero vowed. "I, too, like them, will persevere."

She let her thoughts dance away to frolic with the night.

Outside in the distance a dog was baying.

An Alsatian, she concluded. That handsome duke of dogs.

As though in response to the Alsatian's baying, a dog in the middle distance wailed.

I can't make out this one, Alero pouted, and then decided, "It's a mongrel."

Other mongrels joined in and were soon seized in a tempest of wailing.

"A howling chorus of negativism," Alero muttered to herself. "Like the squealing voices that besiege us daily, telling us we cannot do what we'll in fact do."

Soon the song of the mongrels ended, and she heard, somewhere far away, the long-suffering whine of a scooter bleeding the heart of night.

She jangled the keys of her music cases.

Should I listen to some real music?

No, she thought. Tonight I shall sleep early.

She opened her bedside cabinet and tucked away her keys.

She had begun locking the cases and hiding the keys the day her mother discovered her secret possessions.

She was reading in the living room when her mother came ponderously down the stairs, a strange look in her eyes.

She sat opposite Alero and stared at her.

Alero saw fear in her eyes, and pain. And then intuitively it came to her. *Mom has discovered my CD player!*

She waited in rising panic for her mother to pronounce the dispossessing sentence. But none came. Her mother simply got up, stood still a moment, then began to walk off.

"Never let your Dad find out," she warned, heading back upstairs.

A soft breeze raided the open window and

filled the room with a bouquet of scents.

Someone has just finished having a bath somewhere, Alero mused. I can smell lavender soap. Maybe it's those two, the red-beret-and-blue-dungaree twins.

Don't be silly, she scolded herself, they probably live miles away.

When I'm married I'll have twins.

Will I ever marry?

"Yes," she told the night, "I'll marry and have nine children. No, I'll have five. No, I think I'll have seven, like Uncle Seven. I'm so silly really – I'll just settle for two, like Mom. And they'll be twins. *Oh, I've got twins in the brain!*"

A little tango with mild musings and her mind wandered back to the magazine feature on the ten singers.

They are of the heroic breed, she decided, as she recalled the enormously daunting obstacles they had faced in their climb to self-actualization.

Am I not of the heroic breed?

Her mind went to the night of blood. Wincing, she slammed the picture shut and switched to her talk with Uncle Seven.

"Perhaps you're right, Uncle Seven," she said, half aloud in the dark, "that humanity is clothed in failed dreams. But I do know that every once in a while, some people end up living out their dreams."

Sleep was stealing on her.

"I shall be one of those who end up living out their dreams," she muttered. "I shall be one of those."

Then she slept.

7

Alero laughed. "Mrs. Eguavoen left a description precise to the last pink wriggle of decorating squirt, which must be exactly half an inch to the right of the *Happy Birthday*."

Her mother was running her finger through the order book. "But is it a fruit cake or sponge cake or *what?*"

Alero blinked. "Didn't she say? She was so particular about the details that she insisted on writing everything herself."

Mrs. Lucinda Oti reflected a moment. "I'll make a quarter of it fruit, a quarter sponge, a quarter cheese – and the rest *cassava*." She laughed merrily.

Alero was glad to see her mother laugh.

Her mother had been wrapped in a shawl of sadness when she returned an hour ago.

Even when she announced that Alero's father had been certified OK and was coming home only two days later than scheduled, she had not let up.

And all through lunch, Alero thought, there had been something on the tip of her mother's tongue, which she kept tripping down.

Alero had done all the talking, and had done it with an ease and volubility in run-away contrast not only to her mother's reticence but also to her own painful taciturnity of the last two days.

She had eaten well last night, had slept well, and today, for some unfathomable reason, she was as joyful as a lark at heaven's gate.

"When Brova wakes up, I'll take him with me to Mrs. Eguavoen's to fetch the rest of the order," Alero offered.

"It's a good thing he's asleep," Mrs. Oti remarked, going over to the living room. "I need to concentrate my thoughts. There's something I've been wanting to tell you."

At last, Alero thought. Here it comes.

She joined her mother in the living room and sat facing her.

"They tried to kill your father," Mrs. Lucinda Oti said abruptly.

"*What?*"

"They fiddled with the car. They've tried to get him for ages. You know your father – all that integrity stuff. Twenty-eight years in the Force – and only Chief Superintendent of Police. I've finally got him to see reason – he's retiring."

She paused meditatively.

"An unemployed husband is worth more than a dead police hero." She hesitated, then said bitterly, "A hero slain by one of his own."

The air of sadness that had haunted her returned in double array.

"Things are going to be tough, Alero. My baking can only bring in so much. I've never been a good business person." She looked wistfully at her daughter. "One more reason why I thought Banking and Finance would be more suitable for you. But your father's heart is bent on Medicine."

She cast her sight away dejectedly.

"I've had to give in. It was difficult arguing with the scholarship – especially now that we'd need all the help we can get. But apart from the financial reason, I'd still have had to yield – your father wants you to read Medicine so badly."

She stood up as though to go away.

"All my life I've been giving in to your father, laying my life down for him."

She sat down again and wiped a tear from her eye.

"Twenty-five years ago a seventeen-year-old Trinidadian girl and her parents came down to Nigeria and went to a concert. It was a concert featuring the golden-voiced Flamingo, whose rising fame was coloring the West African coast. The girl met the man who sometimes backed Flamingo on the guitar and piano, and they fell hopelessly in love. He was Flamingo's twin brother. The girl's parents warned her to ditch the Nigerian, but she didn't see any reason for all their fuss – after all, her father had himself married a foreigner – a French Creole. But her father explained that the issue wasn't that her beau was a Nigerian, but that he was a Nigerian police constable on the beat – hardly a suitable match for the Trinidadian ambassador's daughter. But the ambassador's daughter laid down her life for her love – and her parents never spoke to her again."

"So," Alero gasped, "Dad was a twin? Flamingo was my uncle?"

"Your father dreamed of becoming a brain surgeon and he was brilliant and determined enough to achieve it, but he quit school to join the Police Force."

"Why?"

"He needed money to support his brother. The plan was that when Flamingo was sufficiently established as a bandleader, Bawo would go back to school and Flamingo would support him. But Flamingo was never sufficiently established; he was just a flamboyant drain on your father's withering wallet. His life was dames, drink and drugs."

"But the song, the song on television…"

Alero's mind flashed to the song the singer on

TV that night eight years ago had done in Flamingo's version.

Her mother understood.

"Yes," she reflected, "Flamingo had not always been a debauchee. He was once in a church band and had in fact discovered his voice in church." A faraway look came over her eyes. "The burden of his great gift was more than he could bear, I suppose."

Then her eyes suddenly lit up in happy remembrance.

"Your father was also a member of the church band – and a keen church member too. He gave me the first Bible I ever owned. Those were good days."

Mrs. Lucinda Oti was silent a while.

"Everything changed when Flamingo died."

"What happened?"

"He had a crash on a friend's motorcycle. He was stoned – and drunk. He was in coma for six months and your father prayed and prayed. But Flamingo never came out of it. When he died, your father went around mumbling under his breath, 'If only I had been a brain surgeon, if only I had been a brain surgeon...' He mourned Flamingo for one whole year, playing Flamingo's favorite songs on the guitar. Then he tore up all photographs of Flamingo, destroyed other reminders of him and smashed the guitar. He forbade anyone ever to speak of his twin brother. His children were never to know."

She stood up.

"For eight years your father supported Flamingo, hoping he would change. I knew the rascal would never change but I gave up the plans I had of going to university and took up baking to help out. I did this for your father – I laid my life down for him."

She went to the window and stared out.

"Alero..." Mrs. Lucinda Oti's voice cracked

with emotion. "I've agreed that you should study Medicine."

The room sagged under the weight of silence.

Alero stood up. "I'm going over to Mrs. Eguavoen's."

"Aren't you taking Brova with you?"

"No, Mom, I need to be alone."

8

I *dreamed and dreamed in vain, and fruitlessly did I desire,* Alero agonized, trudging with bent head along Sakponba Road.

She had been to Mrs. Eguavoen's and was walking home, having decided not to return by taxi. She needed the walk.

O God, why did you give me my voice? Why did you give me my desire?

She kicked an empty can and sent it skittering into the gutter. She kicked a half-sucked orange. She kicked a dusty corncob.

O God, why? Why did you give me my voice? Why did you give me my desire?

Walking in a daze she bumped into a bread hawker, then into an urchin, then into a Bini chief with anvil haircut and oversized coral beads.

When she bumped into an orange-seller and had to help, amid threats and curses, to retrieve the hawker's oranges from the smelly gutter, she resolved to be more careful.

But anguish had its claws deep in her.

My life is over, she lamented, trundling along. *Over!* Dad is retiring. Money will be hard to come by. I must take up the scholarship. I must study Medicine. I must become a brain surgeon. I must do what my parents want. I must become a brain surgeon. I must study Medicine. I must be grateful for the scholarship. Money will be hard to come by. I must do what my parents want. I must do what my parents want. I must do what my parents want. I must lay down my life…

O God, where are you! Why have you given me pain for sister and anguish for twin? Why have you changed my name to Misery? Why is my middle name Frustration? Why is my surname Hopelessness? Take my life, O God; Take my life and let me die! What use is a miserable, wretched, dreary life? Take my life! Let me die, O God! Let me die!

A face peered into hers.

Begrimed, hairy, shaggy, unkempt, filthy – it was the face of a lunatic.

Alero had halted in her tracks and had been standing still and just staring into nothing, and the lunatic seemed to find this familiar and welcome.

Alero scampered.

I mustn't do that again, she told herself. I promise I won't stand still and just stare into nothing. *It's the way of the mad.*

She kicked an empty sardine can.

Maybe I'm mad and don't know it. O God, help me! I think I'm mad!

She saw another tin can and kicked it. She kicked it again, kicked it yet again, and kept on kicking it till it landed on the size-twelve foot of a man buying *suya* at a roadside grill.

"Sorry!" she shouted to the man, not having yet come abreast. "Sorry! Sorry!"

She kept saying sorry till she came abreast.

When she had gone past, she was still saying sorry.

A spanking new Mercedes Benz car decorated with Christmas lights pulled up to offer her a lift.

"Sorry!" she said, as she had been saying non-stop for the last minute. "Sorry! Sorry! Sorry!"

And the car's hooting and purring and cheap soliciting only met with this one word from the extraordinarily gorgeous teenager with a distracted gaze who deigned to look neither left nor right nor mischievous Benz-ward.

"I've got to lay down my life," she mumbled when the car took its prurience elsewhere. "I've got to lay down my life like Mom does for Dad, and Dad did for Flamingo. I've got to lay down my life for my parents. O God, my life is over and I'm dying, but I'm only sixteen and don't want to die!"

Up ahead a huge procession drifted her way – scores of people, dancing and swaying to drums, holding aloft giant rainbow-colored umbrellas, glinting ornamental scimitars and mysterious boxes overlaid with flashing mirrors.

Huge red coral beads abseiled fat necks to adorn bare and flabby chests; and they danced, the chests – danced in sweat to the behest of beaded wrists brandishing white handkerchiefs. And waists danced too – waists heavy with capacious white wrappers tied arm-thick around proud midriffs.

Alero did a detour.

"We all celebrate our dreams," she moaned, recalling words she had read in Uncle Seven's magazine. "Some the edifices, some the ruins."

Then with a bitter cry, she lamented, "But I'm too young to see the ruins of my dreams. I'm too young!"

O God, why? Why must I die before I have lived?

The day was darkening now, and as Alero plodded along she raised her eyes to the horizon, to the setting sun.

If only, she thought, if only I could disappear with the day into the sunset. If only I could just vanish into the night, and be no more. No more pain, no more feelings, no more knowing, no more anything.

The air suddenly became cool and drops of liquid scouts smacked her face. She could hear the rain coming. It was like the sound of a giant kettle on the boil, great, huge, and awesomely suspended in the sky.

"The rain is still half a minute away," she said. But she was wrong.

The rain hit her immediately and the drops were like lynching stones.

In a minute the streets were deserted, Alero taking all the drenching for everyone. But all that assailed the youngster to any anguish as she squished her way home was: *I must lay down my life...*

*

"Mom, it's a fruit cake Mrs. Eguavoen wants," Alero reported, sloshing through the back door and squelching a sodden way past her mother, who was making supper.

At the sight of her daughter, Mrs. Oti let out a shriek but Alero fled to her room and locked the door.

Lucinda Oti raced up and banged furiously on the door, but Alero yelled that she needed to be alone, she wasn't feeling too well, but it wasn't the rain, Mom; Mom, you can guess what it is (leaving her mother to imagine it was period pains); yes, she was taking off her wet clothes and would dry herself thoroughly and wrap herself up and wouldn't catch a chill; no, she didn't want any supper; no, not even a little salad and strips of barbecued chicken; no, not even a cucumber sandwich or a mug of Horlicks; yes, she would be all right. Oh, you worry about the wrong things, Mom; *I said you worry about the wrong things!* No, I'm not saying any more; I'll be all right, Mom; I'll be fine…

Her mother left reluctantly.

When she came back at about 11 PM and knocked, Alero didn't answer and her mother left again, thinking her daughter was sound asleep.

Mrs. Lucinda Oti was right and wrong, for her daughter was indeed asleep but not soundly.

For Alero at that moment was writhing in deadly combat with Munro the killer dog, and Munro had sprouted a pair of heads and lions' teeth which he used to savage Alero until the skin on her face hung loose like a banana peel – and there was blood everywhere and Alero asked whose blood it was and tried to stick her face back in place but it would not stay and the twins came and lent her their face but Rest Peacefully said we do not permit that here you'd have to stand aside and watch the mannequins take their exams so she went over to play the piano which was on the back of a rather jumpy elephant and Dad whacked her on the head with a guitar that had lost its strings to a frail and frosty fisherman in faraway Trinidad and she cried because she had grown so tall and had to stoop so she wouldn't scrape the ceiling of the sky with the

roof of her head and she peeped through the
hatch and was surprised to find Cinderella home
with Hansel and Gretel and the three bears and
all the while flamboyant Flamingo was flapping
his frilly wings to the drums at the edge of night
and the judge said I sentence you to a life
without music and out of his mouth popped a
machete-wielding Tessy in a sleigh pulled by
two-headed Munro and she couldn't find Brova
even though she looked carefully under the bed
and the bird-man said your throat is in the cage
and she looked in the refrigerator and saw her
heart playing Scrabble with Mom and Mom said
open your mouth and she poured in iodine to
heal the scar which was playing hide-and-seek
with Tessy under the hibiscus shrub by a lake in
Brova's navel where spinsters troop on Sundays
to discuss marriage and sundry loves and she
cried and cried because she couldn't find Brova
in the bookcase hanging from the coconut tree

which Songbird brought Brova from a strange land in a strange storm that rained down strange gold coins and Munro took the girl's red bicycle and rode it with no hands to Trinidad where Dad had found a job on a sugar plantation and Dad snatched the slave-driver's whip which Uncle Seven had carefully hidden in his nose and struck her on her scar and the pain was like ice cream in acid and she ate up all the ice blocks at Sapele motor park and all the while flamboyant Flamingo was flapping his frilly wings to the drums at the edge of night and the killer dog chased her with lions' fangs and a yellow lily and she ran for her dear life and Mom came to call her into the house because she had failed her exams but two-headed Munro caught her and dragged her down and mauled her and chewed her neck and there was blood blood blood everywhere.

Alero slept and didn't sleep, and throughout

the night Munro the killer dog chased her and she couldn't run fast for her life because she had to carry a basinful of blood. And Mom kept on calling her indoors because she had failed her exams. And she cried, but her tears were just soap suds and vinegar…

9

Mrs. Oti rapped on the door. "Aren't you up yet?"

Alero's eyes snapped open and she gasped for breath.

In the fog of emergence from turbulent slumber to terrified wakefulness, her mother's voice reached her like sound wrapped in a paper bag and buried in the trash.

"Mom," she rasped, her eyes popping with fright.

Aww!

Her hand went apprehensively to her face; it was intact. She put her hand to her neck; it was unsavaged.

She looked around, Munro was not crouching in the room poised to tear her to bits. And there was no basin of blood in her hands.

She wiped the sweat from her brow.

"Alero…" her Mom attempted again.

"Mom, *good morning!*"

She raised herself to rest against the bed head, surveying the debris of her trenchant foray into nightmare wonderland.

The sheets were hanging down the foot of the bed, her pillow was in a twisted heap on the floor, and the bed was soaked, soaked, soaked with perspiration.

"Are you still not letting anyone in?" her mother asks.

Alero is still not letting anyone in.

She still needs time to herself, she tells her

mother. Yes, she would be all right while her mother takes Brova out shopping; yes, she would take a good warm bath; yes, she would make herself a nice breakfast; yes, she would stay out of her room for a while to get fresh air.

Mrs. Lucinda Oti, thus assured that all was well on the home front, left Alero to go shopping with Brova.

When Alero was sure her mother had left the house, she jumped out of bed and took a quick bath.

Purposefully selecting the blue designer jeans with the gold threading her mother had given her, she hurriedly slipped it on.

She strode to the wardrobe, yanked out her red suitcase and threw out all the camouflaging clothes, leaving only the CDs.

Lugging the suitcase downstairs, she grabbed the spare front door key from the biscuit tin in the pantry, and trotted out of the house.

Twenty minutes later she was at the old ramshackle music shop on Cooke Road.

The "New and Second-Hand CDs Sold Here" sign needed a paint retouch, Alero mused, but the decrepitude of the shop did not seem to have infected the storekeeper. He had an air a teeny bit too refined for the dilapidation that surrounded him.

In life there are things we cannot explain, Alero concluded. Fishes do sometimes find themselves in birds' nests. And birds in cages, and people too.

"Do you want Aretha Franklin?" she asked the storekeeper.

He grinned at her and rubbed his chest. "I have two wives. Two wives more than my house can handle. Whatever will I do with a third?"

"I mean would you be interested in buying her CDs?"

"Ah, that's an entirely different matter." He

patted his belly. "Let's have a look."

A short while later, Alero was back home to fetch the second batch of goods destined for the storekeeper who had no use for a third wife.

The driver of the taxi she had chartered helped her carry the black suitcase to the cab, and soon she was back at the music shop.

"We all do get a little hard up now and then," said the storekeeper genially, as he handed Alero the money for the CD player and the suitcase.

Alero stuffed the money into a purse already distended with the money he had paid for the CDs and other suitcase.

She squeezed the purse and marched out without a glance at her once most-prized possessions.

A few minutes later, she was at the bird shop.

The Lebanese shopkeeper gazed at her with trepidation, but she forced a smile his way.

"I've come to apologize for my behavior the

other day," she said gaily, "and to buy as many birds as I can afford."

When Alero left the shop, the bird-man shook his head as he contemplated his empty cages, and the birds were in the sky or wheresoever their whims and wings took them.

Stopping at a hardware stall on Cooke Road, Alero bought a razor blade and crossed over to a hairdressing salon near Omon Stores.

She sighed with pleasure when she discovered she was the only customer and could receive immediate attention.

"A quick haircut, please," she said.

The hairdresser took one look at her long and gorgeous hair and cried in astonishment, "You want me to cut this?"

"Yes."

"No! Girls will kill for this hair – and you want me to *cut it?*"

Alero snatched a pair of scissors, grabbed the

base of her hair and snipped.

"There," she smiled. "Now you can do the rest. And make it ultra low, please."

Alero had to endure the tears of the woman, but at last her hair was cropped satisfactorily low.

Asking for the toilet, she was taken to a cubicle in an adjoining building.

"Such lovely hair," the hairdresser wept as she left Alero. "Such lovely hair – gone..."

Alero shut the toilet door, pulled off her jeans and cut the legs of the garment with her blade.

Taking up what was left of her mother's loving gift, a gift her father and everyone truly admired, she scrutinized it.

It had become a pair of head-turning short shorts.

She put the skimpy thing on and walked out to a wolf-whistling world.

When she arrived home, she stood by the

front door listening for sounds in the house. Hearing enough to assure her that her mother was back home, she glued her finger to the doorbell.

She heard her mother hurrying with Brova to the door and braced herself.

The door opened.

Lucinda Oti stared at her inquiringly, then screamed, "Alero!"

Alero stepped into the house and sulked past her mother to the living room. She dropped defiantly into a chair.

Her mother skidded to her. "*What did you do to your hair?*"

Defiant eyes softened to kitty sweetness. "I cut it, Mom."

Brova grinned and clambered on her lap. "You cut your hair."

"I did, didn't I?" Alero hugged and kissed her brother. He smelled nicely of baby oil and bubble gum.

"You cut your hair," her mother whimpered, stifling back tears.

"Yes, I cut my hair," Alero purred.

Mrs. Lucinda Oti could stem her tears no longer. They flowed copiously.

Brova fidgeted on Alero's lap. "Why is Mom crying?"

"I don't know, sweetheart. Why don't you ask her?"

"Mom, why are you crying?" Brova asked.

Mrs. Oti's jaw went slack as she gazed at Alero's bare legs. "And the lovely jeans I bought you – did y-you walk through town *like this?*"

"Don't cry, Mom," Brova told the distraught woman.

Her eyes traveled back to Alero's shorn head. "Your hair, your hair," she sobbed.

Brova climbed down from Alero's lap.

"Sorry, Mom; don't cry, Mom." He ambled up

to his mother and tried to wipe her tears with his little palm.

Noticing that Alero had begun to cry too, he toddled back to her.

"Sorry, Alero; please don't cry; don't cry." He ran his palm over her tears, and then turned back to his mother.

Shuttling back and forth between weeping mother and sobbing sister, the nations of his little world, the little lad sued assiduously for an end to all rifts and tears.

"And I went up to your room," Lucinda Oti wailed. "All your CDs are gone, the CD player…" She stared suspiciously at Alero. "What did you do to them?"

"I sold them, Mom."

"Sold them? W-why?"

"The caged birds had to be set free."

Mrs. Oti sat in bewildered silence, trying to make sense of things.

PHILIP BEGHO

"Alero, what's wrong?" she said finally. "Are you pregnant?"

"Mom!" Alero was horrified.

Her mother pondered a moment. "But is it a boy?"

"You know me better than that, Mom!"

"Then whatever could be wrong!" exclaimed her mother. She hesitated. "Did someone... you know... h-hurt you?"

Alero glared accusingly at her. "I'm going to be a banking surgeon!"

"A banking surgeon?"

"I mean... I mean..."

Alero couldn't say what she meant and broke into the deep sobbing that marks the bereaved.

Hastening to her, Mrs. Oti drew her daughter to her breast, and little Brova tried to embrace them both, tears running down his cheeks.

After a while Lucinda Oti took Alero upstairs to her room.

"I'm g-going to lay down my life, M-Mom," Alero spluttered. "I'm going to lay down my life."

Her mother tucked her in bed and sat silently by her until the sobbing abated.

Brova snuggled into bed too, a protective arm around his big sister.

Mrs. Oti got up. "I won't be a minute."

When she returned, it was with a book. "Have a look at this."

Alero regarded the Bible her mother handed her.

Lucinda Oti gave a wan smile. "It's seven years older than you – a gift from your father. It was the first Bible I ever owned."

Alero sat up, curious to examine this relic of her parents' shadowy past.

She put an arm around Brova, who was now resting against her, eager to share in his sister's inspection of the Bible and all things shareable.

"Turn to Psalm 23," her mother suggested. "Your father taught me to recite that psalm off by heart."

As Alero turned the pages, Mrs. Oti added gravely, "Your father lost his faith when his beloved Flamingo died. He never wanted to see a Bible again and decreed that no such material be found in the house."

She paused, and her voice became even more severe. "It's a dreadful thing to lose one's faith. A most dreadful thing."

Alero found Psalm 23 and read it silently.

At her mother's request she read it aloud, and then read it silently again.

Turning to other pages, she was soon oblivious of the presence of her mother and brother, and surrendered herself to words that strangely seemed to address the yearnings of her secret heart, words that had been hoarded from her too long.

Her mother stood up.

"Come, Brova, let's go down and prepare lunch."

When she returned an hour later with a lunch tray, Alero was still immersed in the Holy Book.

Even when Mrs. Lucinda Oti brought up her daughter's supper much later, Alero had not got tired of reading.

But at about 9 PM when she came to collect the tray, she found that Alero had bathed and was snuggled up, sleeping like a baby.

She gave her daughter a peck on the cheek and left the room humming *What A Friend We Have in Jesus*, which she remembered from her younger days with Bawo Oti, police constable on the beat.

10

Mr. Bawo Oti, Chief Superintendent of Police, soon to retire, eased his back from the dining chair and remarked to his wife that he had never seen Alero look quite so radiant.

From her seat Mrs. Lucinda Oti looked across to the kitchen door.

A smile touched her lips.

"Indeed, there's been a curious glow around her all day," she told her husband.

In a perfect world, it would have given her great joy to come out with the truth and say that God had spoken to Alero as she read the Bible. But her husband's long-standing instructions made such a move quite unwise.

What God had told Alero, Mrs. Oti didn't know, for her husband had returned before the matter could be discussed to any enlightening degree.

"She's been an angel," Lucinda Oti commented, as washing-up sounds reached her through the kitchen door.

Alero had taken up her father's traveling cases, served him a refreshment, prepared and served lunch, cleared the dishes, and now was washing up, with the graceful dispatch that was her accustomed way.

"But I don't understand the hair business," Mr. Oti murmured, a furrow on his brow.

"Oh, it will grow."

Lucinda Oti hoped her off-hand manner would snuff further interest in the matter. But this was not to be.

"Why did she cut it?" her husband demanded.

"She likes it short."

"The truth, Lucinda."

Lucinda sighed. "I suppose it was all the emotional seesaw, darling. Here I was wooing her from Medicine to Banking one day and wooing her back to Medicine the next. There's only so much ebb and tide a tender mind can take."

Bawo Oti patted his full but trim midriff.

"I'm happy we're agreed it should be Medicine. I've always believed in consensus."

"Going up, up, up, into the sky," Brova announced. He was playing a loud airplane game in the living room.

The kitchen door opened and Alero popped her head round.

"What would we be having for supper, Mom? I'd like to know now so I can put out the ingredients and stuff."

"Coming down, down, down, down from the sky!" Brova was quite carried away by his game.

Bawo Oti smiled at his daughter. "I was just telling your mother how glad I am she's agreed with us that Medicine is the right course for you."

Alero smiled back. "I won't be doing Medicine, Dad."

"Crash!" Brova interjected. His Air Force 1 had crashed.

Mr. and Mrs. Oti's eyes popped.

"I-I had no idea I had persuaded you so firmly to Banking and Finance," Alero's mother stuttered.

"I won't be doing Banking and Finance, Mom."

Silence again, sitting grim and tight around

the neck of bewilderment.

Alero's father cleared his throat. "What will you be doing then?"

"I'm going to sing." Alero raised her face to the ceiling and seemed to look through it to the sky. "The Lord has set the captives free. Who can bid the songbird 'Be silent, sing not'?"

She glanced at her father.

"Dad, I was born to sing."

Turning she went into the kitchen, the first notes of a song rising from her bosom.

Mrs. Lucinda Oti, sitting in fearful silence by her husband, stiffened when she realized Alero was singing *Amazing Grace*, rendered in Flamingo's famous version, the version that had been the cause of all the violence eight years ago.

She averted her face from her husband's, but was careful to keep him in the periphery of her vision.

She would pounce like a tigress to restrain him if he made any violent move for the kitchen. He would have to kill her to touch Alero this time.

Alero's singing went into gale force and Brova tossed his precious plane aside and skipped towards the kitchen, the glee of surprise sunny on his face.

He cast a cursory glance at his tense and silent parents, and shot into the kitchen. But he didn't quite shut the door after him and the vaulting beauty of Alero's voice surged out in glorious waves.

A tear crept down Lucinda Oti's cheek.

Surely this was not her daughter singing? Surely it was an angel?

The wonder of it gave Mrs. Oti courage to peek at her husband.

In his hands his head was shaking, his palms covering his face. He removed his hands and stared at his wife. She saw that his eyes were red with unshed tears.

Bawo Oti reached tenderly for his wife's hand, and together they rose and went into the kitchen.

"Amazing Grace!" Alero sang. "How sweet the sound that saved a wretch like me!"

The words of John Newton came forth in melodious majesty, mighty around the golden-voiced girl. It enveloped husband and wife, who stood arm in arm, and brother and sister, with brother cradled in sister's arms.

"Through many dangers, toils and snares I have come," Alero declared. "It's grace that brought me safe thus far, and grace will lead me home."

"O God!" cried Bawo Oti, crashing to his knees. "O God!"

Alero fell silent and regarded her father.

"I have fled you through the years," Bawo Oti

confessed to his Maker, "but you have chased and hunted me down!"

He broke into tears and wept like a child.

Alero passed the cradled Brova to her mother and dropped to her knees by her father, embracing him.

Mr. Oti gazed into his daughter's eyes.

"Forgive me, my daughter," he entreated. "Forgive me, my precious, precious child!"

Overcome, Alero wept with her father.

Mrs. Lucinda Oti hugged the tearful Brova close to her breast.

"Amid a veil of tears hath God visited my home," she whispered through her own tears.

And then she broke down in great sobs.

Sobbing for joy.